From

Texas,

to

Argentina,

to

Antarctica,

and
The
World's
End.

「現實生活中，我往往會避開令我害怕的事。

但跟妳在一起，妳總是讓我做些瘋狂的事，就像我們正在做的這件事，還是在這種地方。

當初我提議南極，純粹是開玩笑，妳卻當真了。

人一生中，有幾件事特別恐怖，跟人告白就是其中一種。

是妳讓我辦到了……。是妳讓我辦到的，但不是因為妳說了什麼，而是因為，妳就是妳。」

——George 的婚禮誓詞／南極／ 2015 年

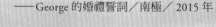

In my real life, I often avoid things that scare me. but not when I'm with you.

You make me do some crazy stuff, including what we're doing now and where we're doing it.

I was kind of kidding when I suggested Antarctica but you just ran with it.

One of the scariest things you can do though, is to tell someone that you love them first.

You made me do that…you made me do that not with words, but by being who you are.

- George's wedding vows; Antarctica 2015

六年級時，Janet 在學校話劇飾演哥倫布，假裝踏上冒險旅程，探尋未知土地。儘管台詞背得亂七八糟，這位不知所云的中學生硬是從災難脫身，表演贏得觀眾起立鼓掌。

好吧，開玩笑的。在場唯一起立鼓掌的，是我爸媽（他們不得不）跟坐在後面幾個大人（因為他們急著要去上廁所）。但這不是重點。重點是，年紀還這麼小，我就選擇了探險家的角色。我想見識見識，這世界有什麼值得一看，也想知道自己有什麼值得展現給大家。

時間快轉，喏！我成了旅遊節目主持人，心甘情願踏上這兩種意義非凡的人生旅程：第一，前往世界的盡頭（南極）；第二，也是更恐怖的（對我來說），是要做出承諾，與某人共度一輩子。我得學習怎麼分享。我到底在說什麼？

許多女生夢想擁有一場完美的白色婚禮，現場有鮮花、白鴿，淚水交織著歡笑，接著是宴會、跳舞……我則幻想要有布萊德·彼特。結果，我的婚禮既沒有布萊德·彼特，也沒有夢幻電影場景，倒是有雪球紛飛、企鵝便便、極地跳水、挖掘墳墓……以及很多很多。我想，以這種方式為我跟 George 的婚姻拉開序幕，再完美不過了。

十歲的我，是個自詡為探險家、熱愛冒險的小女孩，現在和以後的我，也依然如此。唯一不同是，現在我多了個共犯。

In 6th grade, Janet did a school play where she got to dress up as Christopher Columbus and pretend to embark on an adventure to unknown territories. She messed up her lines catastrophically but then somehow, managed to find her way back from the muddled mess of middle school nonsense words and deliver a standing ovation worthy performance.

Ok, who am I kidding. The only people giving me a standing ovation were my parents (because they had to) and a couple adults in the back (because they had to go pee really badly). But that's all beside the point. The important thing is that even from when I was just a kid, I had always chosen the role of explorer. I wanted to see what the world could show me and what I could show the world.

Fast forward and voila - I'm a travel show host ready to embark on two journeys of a lifetime: first one, to the end of the world (Antarctica), and second, even more scary (for me), a commitment to spend the rest of my life with somebody else. I was going to have to learn how to share. WHAT?

While many girls dream of having the perfect white wedding with flowers, doves, tears and laughter, followed by banquet and dance… I dreamed of Brad Pitt. Instead of Brad Pitt and a dreamy movie-like wedding though, I got snow ball fights, penguin poop, polar plunging and grave digging… and….I can't think of a better way to start my marriage with George.

I will always be that 10-year old little girl who considers herself an explorer and lover of adventure. The only difference now, is that I have a partner in crime.

Janet Hsieh ———

謝怡芬

George Young

吳宇衛

When a seven year old George was given a homework assignment to predict what he'll be when he grew up, George wrote that he'd be a stand-up comedian by the time he was 25. He drew an incredibly detailed picture that illustrated this prophecy: George standing on a stage, in front of what looked like tens of people. Said picture was deemed by both the Louvre and New York's Museum of Modern Art to be "of inadequate significance to be even considered for submission".

With such a vividly illustrated prediction avowed at such a young age, I - George Young - naturally became a lawyer instead.

But I always had this hankering to entertain. A little voice in my head convinced me that - although I grew up with absolutely no one in my (admittedly small) social circle of acquaintances who could confirm this to be the case - I could make some semblance of a living reciting someone else's writing in front of an audience and/or camera.

And so, with only my hair gel and a smile, off I went to pursue a little boy's dream to be on the big screen.

Along the way I bumped into this girl Janet; she fell head over heels with me (almost literally: I had to catch her mid-faint during our first meeting - more on that later) and, several food and coffee dates later, we've reached the end of our single days, and the beginning of all this adventuring that I hope isn't a taste of things to come (I'm a homebody who likes to play with tech and video games when all is said and done...I'm also a poet who just doesn't know it, and I like to write about myself, for no other reason than because it is fun).

七歲時，George 被交代一份回家作業，題目是要預測自己長大後會成為怎樣的人。當時我寫道，二十五歲時要當脫口秀喜劇演員，還畫了一張畫，鉅細靡遺描繪了這項預言：我站在舞台上，台下大概有數十名觀眾。從藝術評論家的觀點來看，這幅畫「毫不值得一提，不必浪費時間毛遂自薦」，無論羅浮宮或現代藝術博物館都看不上眼的。

於是，我，George Young，成了一名律師。

不過，我的表演欲未曾削減。儘管長大過程中，小到不能再小的社交圈裡沒人看好自己，但腦海總有個細微的聲音告訴著我：總有一天，我能靠在鏡頭前唸台詞，勉強糊口飯吃。

於是，就憑著髮膠和招牌笑容，我頭也不回追逐兒時編織的大銀幕夢想。半途中，遇到了 Janet 這女孩，她死心塌地愛上了我（此話不假：第一次碰面，要不是我伸手扶她，她早就昏倒在地），後來經過幾次美食與咖啡約會，我們總算雙雙結束了單身，一起踏上這趟驚險萬分的冒險之旅，但願這不是未來的預兆啊（再怎麼說，我都是愛研究 3C、打遊戲的阿宅……還是個文人騷客只是不自知……還愛寫些關於自己的東西，沒別的原因，純粹好玩）。

Chapter. 01

兩個人的旅途
A Journey for Two

踏上旅途前，
旅程早已展開

很久以前我就想去南極，最早是跟媽媽去阿根廷最南端的城市烏斯懷亞（Ushuaia），我們在港口看見許多從那裡要出航到南極大陸的船隻，當時我跟媽媽就說好，這一生一定要去南極一次。一年前這件事再次被提起，媽媽想參加旅行團去南極，我看了一下行程覺得很無趣！當下問 George 的意見，沒想到他竟然開玩笑說：「我們乾脆在那結婚吧。」

於是我們開始作功課，發現南極有一個俄羅斯東正教的三一教堂（Trinity Church），George 是希臘東正教徒，而且這座教堂就位在「喬治王島」（King George Island）上，對於這樣的巧合，我們兩個都覺得很欣喜，這正是適合我們結婚的地方！

Ⓖ 我們籌備這趟旅行時，並沒有真的發生什麼「爭執」；確切來說，一旦我們決定好要到南極之後，Janet 就開始打點所有的事。

Ⓙ 有啦我們有一些爭執，我覺得你想東想西，不夠果決，一直想著如果你這時剛好有電影的工作進來怎麼辦……

Ⓖ 還好啦，這趟旅行出發前我們並沒有真正有什麼爭吵，都是討論的成份比較大。

Ⓙ 我來解說一下剛才我們對話的背景。其實我們這次出去之前確實有爭吵，因為如果單純是結婚的話就只要十幾天就好了，但是因為還搭配了工作要製作成一個節目，旅程就從德州、阿根廷一路走到了南極半島。George 是演員，不是旅行節目主持人，這是我的節目，而對他來說他等於是放掉五十幾天的工作來成就我的工作。我們有一些爭執，但也不是真的大吵的那種，比較像是溝通的過程。

共同的旅程開始之前，
自己一個人旅行的光景

Ⓙ 我在旅行的時候總是喜愛找人攀談、尋找新鮮的事物、總是想要冒險、總是想要走在蹊徑上，對我來說這才是旅行真正有趣的事情！我不斷尋找機會挑戰，也不斷地想嘗試新的事物。

Ⓖ 我旅行的時候，喜歡看書，喜歡待在飯店裡；我也喜歡比較舒適甚至有點奢華的事物。大致上而言，旅行的時候我喜歡舒適勝過花力氣探索、發掘，喜歡安全的地方，當我必需出門去工作、拍戲的時候我出門，工作結束後就回到舒適的地方，窩在自己的洞穴天地裡面……我並不介意偶爾走出去看看，但不需要這麼做的時候，不會特別去追求「探索」這件事。

Ⓙ 他在英國的家離巨石陣才 20 分鐘車程，但是從來沒去過！他之前在印度工作的時候，我們照例會通 Skype，我一直推薦他要去某些景點、推薦美味的料理，但他最後是在飯店房間裡面點餐哈哈哈！

Ⓖ 所以說南極並不是我心目中旅行目的地的首選，阿根廷、德州也差不多。

Ⓙ 南極又冷又沒網路，德州、阿根廷的行程中他要騎馬、泛舟、搭直昇機，這些都是危險的事。

Ⓖ 但是我是演員，所以在電視上看起來還蠻安然自在，好似一個熱愛冒險的人哈哈！不過我在攝影機前面並不將自己塑造成動作片英雄那樣的形象，我還是經常對著攝影機嚷嚷自己覺得危險，也會坦率地承認自己有些懼怕。我並不嚮往旅行，更沒想過這樣的旅行。但實際上，為了工作我經常在旅行。有時在美國、有時在新加坡、倫敦、台灣……，我並不介意為了工作旅行，但是身為一個並不嚮往旅行的人卻有著飛行的命運，這是人生奇妙之處。

不止是旅程——
更是人生風景

我一直在旅行，無論是工作或者是自己旅行，或者是自己的旅行變成工作的一部份，這是我從以前到現在的生活。

以前我們也曾一起旅行過，是真正一起去玩，不像這次的結婚之旅帶有一些工作的成份。過去兩個人的旅行，有時是我們其中一方要工作，另一方剛好有空檔，就會飛去陪伴，只有一方在工作，是一種陪伴的心情。這次一起旅行，更像是一起工作，只要在一起就是一起工作，並沒有真的有這麼多私下的相處時間。

到了南極之後比較有時間，最重要的原因就是上船後有三十幾個小時不能進行拍攝，所有工作人員都嚴重暈船，紛紛嘔吐！但我們兩個沒有，因此得到了小型的假期，而且我們還打賭喔，兩人約好上船前不吃暈船藥，看誰先受不了，所以我們兩個一路上都想：「他（她）沒有吃之前，我才不要吃！」就這樣逼迫自己，最後竟然兩個人都沒事。

George 在旅行的想法與我十分不同，也許乍聽之下我們在開始旅行前、在旅途中會因為想法非常不同而有許多爭吵，實際上並非如此。無論 George 平常如何不嚮往

旅行，他永遠都保持著願意嘗試的胸懷，就算再不甘願，他就算邊抱怨，最終也是願意跟我一起嘗試的。

這就是我非常願意與他一起旅行甚至是一起走在人生的旅途上的原因。如果他既害怕又不願意放手嘗試，我們也許就不會在一起了。我們從認識到談戀愛，歷經了十年的友情，各自在生命裡有許多轉折與變動，才結為夫妻。我們是如此不同的人，人生的各種遭遇讓我們在十年後成為適合彼此，卻又這麼不同的人。所以，在旅途開始之前，我們早就已經花了十年的時間，將自己準備好要一起走過下一個十年、二十年或更長久了！

Ⓖ 與 Janet 一起旅行，我得以去到很多我自己一個人不曾想過要去的地方，她鼓勵甚至是促使我探索了許多新的地方以及新的事物。當然我並不是一個完全對新的事物不好奇的人，自己旅行的時候還是會遊歷一些地方，但與她在一起，我得到了很多前所未有的經驗，這是一個人旅行的時候辦不到的事情。嗯，跟旅遊節目主持人結婚還是不錯的！

Ⓙ （眨眼）你以前有跟其他女孩一起去旅行過吧！差別在哪？

Ⓖ 嗯⋯⋯主要還是她們想要出去旅行，我大部份想的還是找個不錯的餐廳之類的事⋯⋯。

Ⓙ 才不是呢！你帶她們去過巴黎，登上艾菲爾鐵塔；你也帶女孩子去過希臘⋯⋯。

Ⓖ 還是她們想去啦，她們帶領我旅行⋯⋯。

南極之旅
是怎麼成行的？

by Janet

我一向愛作夢。只要能採取行動、付諸實踐，我並不覺得愛作夢有什麼不好。有夢就去追。

二〇一一年，我到阿根廷拍攝旅遊節目。收工後，和母親、製作人利用幾天假期，飛去全球最南端的城市烏斯懷亞。那幾天，有好幾艘遊輪在我們眼前駛離碼頭、開往南極——白色大陸、第七大陸、企鵝國度。我好羨慕。羨慕死了。好想跳上其中一艘，躲進衣櫃，或應徵船上的侍者或服務生。我好想好想去南極。但天啊，結果那年、隔年、後年都未能成行。烏斯懷亞有幾個外島，我們跨了好幾個島，企鵝看個夠，要不是企鵝身形小又滑不溜丟的，真想偷渡一隻回家（說說而已）。

又過幾年，爸媽退休，決定找朋友一同搭遊輪去南極，問我要不要跟，還把行程寄給我。一看到行程跟價目表，我立刻打通電話給爸媽，要他們趕緊把訂位退了。價

位太高，遊覽機會太少，實際待在南極大陸的時間也少得可憐。我認為我可以當他們的導遊，幫他們挑個較舒適又實惠的遊輪。

兩週過後，我買了兩本旅遊書，牆上貼了張南極地圖，寫電子郵件給全球十數間船舶經營商。身懷重任，這趟旅程勢在必行。這期間，George 和我已經開始約會了，我除了和他分享這件事之外，自然也邀他同行。

George 和我不同，不愛冒險，寧可舒舒服服躺在沙發，讀讀旅遊書或看看節目，也不願參加風險四伏、危機重重的異國旅行，所以，我知道說服他很難。於是，我改用開玩笑的口吻說，既然我都邀他了，他不如也找他爸媽一起來，畢竟大家住在地球兩端，平時相處的時間也不多。

沒想到，George 竟玩笑似的說：既然我們

爸媽都難得能相聚，又從沒碰過面，我們未來在一起的時間又多的是，既然難得邀他們同行，不如乾脆就在南極把婚結一結了。

George 並不知道，這番話從此在我心中生根萌芽了，什麼都阻攔不了我。他早該知道，這類點子一旦進我腦袋，就會持續醞釀，直至夢想成真。決定了，我就要在南極結婚。但願到時候，George 仍會是我的新郎。

幸運的是，稍微用 Google 搜尋了一下，發現南極有個教堂，而且是在喬治王島（譯註：該島英文名稱為 King George Island）上。沒錯，正是「喬治」王島。島上有個俄羅斯東正教教堂，而 George 正是受洗的東正教基督徒。簡直是天注定。

接下來，想當然就要對 George 動之以情了。我告訴他，喬治王島有這麼一個教堂，恰符合我們的意——這就是所謂的命中注定。果然有效。嗯，勉強算是，起碼有誘他上鉤。憑我的三寸不爛之舌，費了數禮拜的工夫，才總算慢慢把他變成我的甕中鱉。嗯哇哈哈哈。

至於這趟旅程和婚禮究竟如何成真，又是另一段極為漫長的故事了：過程充滿頭疼、淚水、爭吵、沮喪、失望、憤怒……各種糟糕的情況也都發生了。開玩笑的啦。當然還是有期盼、興奮、躍躍欲試、這是夢嗎拜託捏我一把的時刻；短短幾年前，這一生難及的夢想，似乎只是一個遙不可及的目標，如今美夢成真，此刻更有一種無與倫比的滿足。

所以，就算 George 打死不承認，我們之所以會在南極結婚，基本上就是他的錯。而對於他當初犯下的錯，我一輩子心存感激。①

How did this trip come to be?

by Janet

I've always been a dreamer. And I don't think that's a bad thing to be, as long as you actually do something about your dreams. Make your dreams a reality.

In 2011, I filmed a travel show in Argentina. After we finished, I took a few days off with my mom and producer and we flew down to Ushuaia, the southernmost city in the world. For a few days, we watched as several cruise ships left the dock and headed for Antarctica, the White Continent, the 7th Continent, Penguin-Land. I was jealous. So so jealous. I wanted to jump onto every single one of those cruises and hide in the closet, or get hired as a valet/server on the ship. I really wanted to go to Antarctica. But alas, it wasn't to be that year, or the next or the next. We got our fill of penguin sighting on a few islands just off of the coast of Ushuaia. I tried sneaking one back home with me, but penguins are quite slippery little things. (I didn't really).

A few years later, my mom and dad, retired, decided that they wanted to go on a cruise to Antarctica with their friends and they asked me if I wanted to join them, sending me their itinerary. One look at the schedule and the costs and I immediately called them up to cancel their reservations. Their booking was way too expensive for way too little excursion and actual time on Antarctica. I would be their tour guide and find them a better cruise for a better value.

Two weeks later, I find myself with two guide books, a map of Antarctica taped to my wall, and emails with at least 10 different ship operators from all over the world. I was on a mission and now, I wanted to go on this trip. George and I were already dating by this point and I wanted to share this experience with him too, so naturally, I invited him to come.

George isn't like me - he doesn't seek out adventure, doesn't like to throw himself at potentially risky and dangerous trips to exotic places. He prefers to read or watch about them from the comforts of his couch, so I knew this would be a hard sell. As a joke, I mentioned that since he was invited, he should also invite his parents since we don't get to spend much time with our parents anymore, with us and them being on the opposite sides of the world.

George surprisingly joked that since we would have both our parents there (who had never met each

other), and since we would have a lot of time together, we might as well get married in Antarctica.

Without knowing it, George had just planted a seed that was resistant to everything. He should have known that an idea like that - once it goes into my brain - is going to fester and fester in there until it happens. I was going to get married in Antarctica. And hopefully, George would be able to join me for our wedding.

As luck would have it, with a little Google search, I had discovered that there was actually a church in Antarctica and on King George Island. Yes, King GEORGE island. And it was a Russian Orthodox church, and George is actually a baptized Orthodox Christian. It was a sign from the heavens.

And of course, playing on George's vanity, I told him about the church on King George Island and how it was just perfect - it was meant to be. It worked. Sorta. I still needed a few more weeks of convincing but I had him on a hook and he was slowly getting reeled into my net. Mwa ha ha ha.

The process of actually making this trip and the wedding happen is a much much longer story: full of headaches, tears, arguments, frustration, disappointment, anger…and then there was all the bad stuff that happened too. Just kidding. Of course, there was the anticipation, the excitement, the build up, the pinching-myself-is-this-really-happening moments, and the satisfaction of actually working towards a dream, a goal, that only a few years ago seemed like such a distant once-in-a-lifetime wish.

Basically, George won't admit it, but it's actually his fault that we ended up getting married in Antarctica. And it's a fault that I will always thank him for. Ⓙ

這是前言
It's a Foreword

by George

起初純粹只是個玩笑。

Janet 和我訂婚之後，難免會討論到何時何地結婚之類的。我嘻嘻哈哈提到（請注意是嘻嘻哈哈），既然我們都沒去過南極，就連 Janet 主持旅遊節目多年也沒去過，那麼，何不就在那結婚呢？

本來以為 Janet 只是聽聽而已。千金難買早知道。

問題得到解答後，往往只會延伸出更多問題：首先，我們要怎麼去南極？要找誰一起去？婚禮要錄影下來嗎？何不乾脆整趟旅程都記錄下來？你覺得這樣總共要花多少錢？

就在這時，探索頻道出現了，聽到我們（我說「我們」，但其實是 Janet、Janet 經紀人李景白和他經營的動能意像製作公司）提出這個想法，覺得很有意思，想在頻道上播出我們的旅遊經歷。

多了有力靠山後，其他就漸漸水到渠成了。故事主線涵蓋 Janet 和我從台北啟程到德州、阿根廷終抵南極，分成數集來拍，南極之旅只會是其中一部分。故事概要：Janet 帶我認識她青少年時期待過的地方，最後在冰天雪地的南極與我共結連理。其他的，我就不爆雷了。

我跟 Janet、攝影團隊從未一同踏上如此長的旅程——短短五十多天要跨越數洲，最後要航行穿越地球盡頭。誰會幹這種事？

人家說，婚後，無論是好是壞，都要守著彼此。結束在桃園機場的拍攝，就要搭機前往第一個目的地：德州休士頓——Janet 的故鄉，也是準岳父母住的地方。頭髮還殘留些許定型液，腦海裡早已盤據一個念頭：這趟遠行對 Janet 和我來說究竟是好是壞。 Ⓖ

It started off as a joke.

Soon after Janet and I got engaged, there was the inevitable discussion about the whens and wheres. I jovially mentioned (please note the joviality) that neither of us had been to Antarctica - even in all Janet's years as a travel show host - so why not get married there?

I wasn't expecting Janet to run with the idea, but then again I should've really known better.

As is the case with all answered questions, more questions arose from its ashes: how would we get to Antarctica in the first place? Who would be coming with us? Should we capture the wedding on video? Why not document the entire journey? How much did you say all this was going to cost?

And that's where Discovery came in - we (I say "we" but really it was Janet, Janet's manager Tim and his Vision Creator production company) pitched the idea to them, and they thought it was such a lovely idea that wanted to air it on their channel.

With the backing of a network in place, everything else started to come together. The journey to Antarctica was to be covered as part of a multi-episode story arc that would take Janet and I from Taipei, to Texas, to Argentina and finally Antarctica. With a basic concept of Janet introducing me to some of the places where she spent some of her formative years in place, we'd ultimately emerge from the cold as husband and wife. No spoilers.

But Janet and I and the film crew had never before undertaken such an extensive journey - we'd all be travelling multiple continents over the span of 50 days, and sailing past the End of the World. Who does that?

They say marriage is for better or for worse; whether Janet and I would emerge better or worse for taking this expedition was looming over our lightly hairsprayed heads as we finished off our final scene in Taipei's Taoyuan Airport, and boarded the plane to our first destination: Houston, Texas - Janet's hometown, and the residence of my future in-laws.
Ⓖ

Dec. 24

愛之旅，從德州老家開始

對我來講，聖誕節是很大的節日，我好久好久沒有回休士頓過聖誕節了！算起來這應該是 George 第二次跟我一起回休士頓，也是我第一次帶他回去過聖誕節。我們一抵達德州之後，隔天就有行程，當天晚上一到我家我們就各忙各的，有人分配房間有人整理器材。

我很喜歡當天的那種感覺，一般出外景就是到飯店之後解散回各自房間，不會有什麼交集，更不可能有什麼家裡的感覺。但是那一天就是真的住在我家裡，我就是一個主人幫大家安排瑣事，我們家也成為這趟旅程的一個基地。我媽媽很開心我們來，她是一個很愛熱鬧的人，所以我們把沙發區清空，就像小時候有同學來家裡 sleep-over 的感覺，然後把每個人安排好，真的很有趣。

那一天晚上是聖誕夜，所以我所有家人都來了，每個人都準備 potluck 一人一道菜，我家也準備了一大堆菜，每個人都吃得很開心，這也是第一次介紹我最喜歡的德州—墨西哥（Tax-Mex）料理給拍攝團隊，它不是德州菜也不是墨西哥菜，但就是一種混在一起的風格，最有名的墨西哥料理其實是德州來的，這是團隊們沒有接觸過的食物風格。

等待酒足飯飽，入夜之後玩的遊戲是「White Elephant」，每人帶一份包裝好的禮物放在一起，然後照順序抽禮物，遊戲規則是，如果你喜歡另一個人抽到的禮物，你就有權力把它搶過來，等所有人抽完禮物，最後留在你手中沒有被搶走的那個禮物就是你的。於是我們開始玩，你偷我的、我偷他的，就這樣偷來偷去，我們甚至為了搶某人的禮物開始聯盟，心機很重地就是要偷到某個東西，很開心很好笑。這也是 George 第一次玩 White Elephant，他很驚訝為什麼我們家玩遊戲可以這麼瘋？因為在他的印象中，玩遊戲一定是很有禮貌的「你想要這個東西？好，我給你」；但我們不是，一直搶來搶去，但是他也笑到不行 Anyway 這就是我們家的風格！那天我們一路玩下去，即使隔天一早就要搭飛機出發到 El Paso，但我們幾乎忘了睡……

這趟旅程的第一晚就在平安夜的溫馨、歡樂氣氛中渡過了，這是我第一次帶 George 在德州過聖誕節，也是第一次認識我這麼多家人！我們已經準備好，從「家」啟程，繼續往另一個家前進！

和團隊
共度聖誕

by George

時值二〇一四年聖誕節，再不久就要踏上五十天左右的旅程，遊歷全球幾個代表景點，那時的我們對旅程的一切都還很新鮮，不像從南極回來後，有種曾經滄海難為水的感覺。

儘管如此，不代表我就不想去親切好客的人家，身邊圍繞著 Janet 的家人、同事、朋友、美食。

我、Janet 和工作團隊從台北出發，歷經十四小時終於抵達她休士頓的老家，一夥人背了大約十三個旅行袋，裝滿衣物、攝影設備、一台無人機（早知道就給它取個名字了）和一堆硬碟。

時差關係，大家原本都沒精打采，累得兩眼通紅，一來到 Janet 老家，燈火通明，暖氣繚繞，加上食物飲料應有盡有，所有人不禁都眼睛一亮，立刻有回到家的感覺。

伯母在前門招呼我們進來，從頭到尾都笑容滿面，最令她開心的，大概莫過於看到小女兒回家了。就算上次見面才在不久之前，母親看到兒女總是笑得最為開懷。

Sally 看見 Janet 開心的程度自不在話下，相較之下，我只是個「碎肝臟」（譯註：英文俚語，喻容易被忽略的人）。我一直覺得，這些年來，「碎肝臟」這名詞老是被人冠上臭名，所以我這裡引用此詞，是帶有一種正面的比喻。不過，作為一個母親，看到自己兒女自然比較開心，這是我比不上的。

進門之後，我們來到餐桌邊，台味德州式家常菜琳琅滿目。苦瓜湯是我的最愛，再加上德州式墨西哥烤肉簡直絕配。沒有火雞（真正的聖誕節還沒到）。

住在休士頓的謝家似乎全體總動員：堂兄弟姊妹、叔叔伯伯、姑姑嬸嬸……一個不

少，全員到齊慶祝台灣家人歸來──當然還有我這個極力和大夥打成一片的假台灣人，誰叫我這樣才能心安理得享用美食點心、欣賞聖誕樹、有個棲居之所。

飽餐一頓後，聖誕節遊戲時間到了，名稱叫做「白象交換禮物」，我也是直到那天才清楚遊戲規則。此遊戲別稱為「洋基人的交換禮物」……聽起來有點種族歧視，但應該沒有吧？（加上問號，因為我真的不確定，而若對洋基人有冒犯之處，容我先道個歉）。

如果你跟當時在休士頓的我一樣，對白象交換禮物一無所知，就讓我告訴你吧，首先最重要的是：跟大象毫無關聯。

這個詞，很明顯是借用英文裡有關「大象」的片語，意思是「食之無味，棄之可惜的禮物」（英文裡也會用大象來形容，房裡的人都覺得某話題有點尷尬，卻又沒

人敢點出來……看來，可憐的大象跟碎肝臟一樣，都被人汙名化了）。

現在，就讓我教你白象交換禮物怎麼玩：

帶包裝好的禮物來派對；
跟大家帶來的禮物放成一堆；
輪下一位時，他有兩種選擇：從禮物堆中挑一個，或「搶奪」前一個人拆開的禮物。

等大家都輪完，禮物也被挑選一空，遊戲便宣告結束。

所以，務必記住一件事，遊戲重點在於，搬上檯面（以當晚來說，就是 Janet 老家的客廳地板）的禮物必須是價值低廉，而且最好是俗不可耐。我得承認，當時我實在擔心自己從台灣帶來的禮物（老實說是 Janet 幫我挑的，我對於送禮這件事完全不在行）有點太過俗氣，而且不只是沒什麼實用性，應該說是毫無用處。

我帶什麼禮物來謝家？牙刷架。牛仔形狀的牙刷架。

不用說，看到 Janet 的堂弟挑到我的禮物時，我著實縮了一下。他本來還面露些許期待（但請別忘了，這些禮物本來就不可能有多好），後來顯然發現我表情「怪怪的」，直到拆開禮物，發現藏在裡頭的東西後，他面色帶有一絲遺憾。

「喔，天啊⋯⋯是牙刷架，」我說，看到他拆開最後一張包裝紙，動作小心翼翼，以這樣的禮物來說，實在令人汗顏。

「喔，謝謝你，」Janet 的堂弟勉強擠出一句話來，「這真不錯──可以拿來用耶，妳說是不是？」他對老婆說，她熱切點頭回應，於是，兩人都很有默契點了點頭。這跟整個故事沒有太大關聯，但我確實看到這畫面，就加減記錄下來了。

「不客氣，」雖然大家都清楚，他的道謝我實在承受不起，我還是立刻回應了。

可想而知，沒人跳出來搶走那份禮物。

究竟，那一晚妙趣橫生的聖誕遊戲中，最棒的禮物是什麼？一組令人驚嘆的棉花糖空氣槍。送禮的不是別人，正是收到我牙刷架的那位堂弟。

我想，最糟禮物獎應該頒給我。幸好，最糟禮物獎的獎品，不是牛仔形狀的牙刷架，謝天謝地。 Ⓖ

Christmas with the Team

by George

Christmas 2014 was very near the start of our fifty day or so trip around significant parts of the world, so perhaps we weren't all as weary and as seasoned as we have since become having emerged from the bottom of the planet.

All this didn't mean however that the feeling of being in a warm, friendly house, filled to the brim with Janet's family, co-workers, friends and food wasn't welcomed by me.

Janet, the team and I had just arrived in the Houston family house from a fourteen hour trip from Taipei. We had around thirteen bags of luggage with us, containing clothing, camera equipment, a drone which in retrospect we really should've named, and a bunch of trusty harddrives.

We all were very likely jetlagged and certainly groggy when we entered Janet's parent's abode - so seeing the place lit up, heated, friendly, and well stocked with food and drink was a sight for sore red eyes for all of us.

Janet's mum was first to welcome us as we passed the front door - she's always smiley, but perhaps seeing her youngest daughter again - no matter how recent the previous meeting was - brings a bigger smile on a mother than anything else can elicit.

I was of course chopped liver compared to Sally seeing Janet, but I personally believe that chopped liver has received a bad rep over the years, and am therefore using this diced organ analogy in a positive way. Nevertheless, I still quite rightly couldn't compare to a mother seeing their own child.

Once we were all inside, we proceeded to the food and drink: lots of Taiwanese-influenced home cooked selections: bitter melon soup being the one I engaged the most in, next to some Tex-Mex fajitas thrown in for good measure. No turkey here (but then again it wasn't yet Christmas Day).

It seemed as if the entirety of the Hsieh Houston Chapter were there that evening: cousins, uncles, aunties...all there to celebrate the return of their Taiwanese family. And then there was me - who was perfectly willing to be as Taiwanese as they needed to be so that I could enjoy the food and refreshments and Christmas tree and roof over my head.

Filled to the brim, we all settled down to a Christmas game that I was - until that day - unfamiliar with: White Elephant Christmas Gift Exchange, aka: Yankee Exchange...which sounds like it should be racist but I guess isn't? (Adding the question mark there to indicate my genuine uncertainty about this and apologies in advance if I've offended any Yankees out there).

For those of you who are as similarly unfamiliar with this Elephant Game as I was that day in Houston, first and foremost: there are no real elephants involved. The term apparently derives from the nickname a gift is given that is hard to get rid of (much like how an elephant is used to describe a potentially awkward topic that everyone in the room is aware of but does not explicitly blurt out to the others;poor elephants almost get as bad a rep as chopped liver).

Here's how you play this White Elephant Gift Exchange game:

Bring one wrapped present to the party;

Place that present in a pile with the other gifts brought by the other peeps at said party;

Take turns picking out any of the gifts that weren't your own and open it. If you're all playing the game properly, the gift will be of a set low value and not at all that useful;

The person next in line then either chooses to pick out another gift from the pile, or 'steal' the already-chosen gift unwrapped by the previous player.

The game's typically over when everyone's had a go and all presents are picked from the pile.

Now - remember that an important part of this game is that the presents you bring to the table (or in this case: Janet's parents' living room floor) are of a low value, and generally pretty kitschy. I must admit I was more than a little concerned that the present that I brought to the game all the way from Taiwan (that Janet admittedly helped me choose as I'm useless at deciding on presents for people) was going to be a little too kitschy, and just past the 'low-use' threshold to 'absolutely pointless'.

My gift to the Hsieh household? A toothpaste holder; a toothpaste holder in the shape of a cowboy.

Needless to say - I cringed as I saw Janet's cousin pick up my present. Evidently he saw my 'tell', as his face changed from mildly pleasant anticipation (remember these gifts were not expected to be amazing to begin with) to regret as he proceeded to discover what lay in store for him.

"Oh god…it's a toothpaste holder," I remark as he unfolds the final piece of wrapping paper with care that was really undeserving of the present within it.

"Oh. Thank you," Janet's cousin manages to get out, "this is really nice - we could definitely use this, couldn't we?" He nods to his partner, who enthusiastically nods in turn, so that their respective nods proceed in sync. This doesn't add to the story admittedly; I just wanted to add that bit of detail in as I did notice that phenomenon.

"You're very welcome," came my automated reply to the thank you that we all knew was not fully deserved.

Predictably, not one person jumped up to steal my gift.

Best gift from that wonderful, Christmas-themed evening? A pair of awesome, marshmallow-shooting air rifles. Donated by none other than the cousin who received my toothpaste holder.

I think I won on the Worst Gift prize. The prize for bringing the Worst Gift? Not a toothpaste holder shaped like a cowboy, thankfully. Ⓒ

對上邊防人員——
反之亦然

by George

我常會過度說明事情。每次我解釋太多，Janet 就會提醒我，而且很常發生。就像此刻，我發現為了說明自己常解釋太多，不知不覺又解釋個沒完。

我這人一向竭盡所能提供資訊。之前在法律事務所擔任實習律師，每次寫電子郵件給委託人，為了解釋原因理由，信件內容總是落落長的，律師、委託人都覺得我給太多資訊了，他們根本不想聽。

早在當時，我就該學到教訓：不論什麼問題，大家都只想聽簡短有力的答案，就算根本沒有這種東西。但，我實在做不到。任何問題進了我腦袋，就會像瀉藥一樣，令我滔滔不絕、「口頭腹瀉」。你看吧，我根本不必再提什麼口頭腹瀉，意思就很明白了。真是抱歉。

也就因為如此，才會衍生後來這件事。在德州的那段期間，我這種過度雞婆回答問題的個性，差點害我觸法。

時值聖誕夜，Janet、攝影團隊和我搭白色小廂型車，準備從休士頓前往馬法鎮。上車前，我還問工作人員，那裡很靠近墨西哥國界，需不需要帶護照，

「當然不用啊，」對方回答。「我們又沒要離開美國。」

聽來十分有道理，於是我樂得把護照留在住處。等大家上了車，我立刻倒頭就睡。好幾個小時過後，聽到聯邦邊防人員的聲音才醒來，他要我們出示護照。

坐在一點都不舒服的車子座椅打數小時瞌睡（這種感覺你也知道，就是頭頸分離，身體又被安全帶繫著猶如戲台上懸絲木偶），被警察猛一敲窗才醒來，立刻感到一陣恍惚。

就在此刻，我才發現，大家幾乎都隨身攜帶護照：主要是因為，對台籍工作人員而言，護照是他們唯一附照片的證件。

除了在下我，還有一個人沒帶護照，那就是 Janet。不過，她身為美國公民，有道道地地的美國腔、德州身分證，如假包換，而我則是純正英國腔，加上才剛醒來，腦袋還不停思索：難道我們跨越了墨西哥國界不成？

「先生，請出示你的護照，」邊防人員大吼（他用脅迫的口吻，「請」跟「先生」二詞純粹是假象）。

「我有美國加州駕照……」

瞧，我的回答簡單明瞭，事情本來可以就此打住的。但不幸的是，接下來我所做的，既不簡單又不明瞭，所以……事情才要開始呢。

「……但我不是美國公民，」我雞婆補一句，口吻略為虛弱，帶有濃濃英國腔。「我來是用簽證。」

「那你的簽證呢，先生？」邊防人員問道，就在這時，廂型車後面走出另一名邊防人員。

「在我護照裡，」我如此答道。只見現場氣氛漸漸尷尬了起來，腦袋才稍醒了些。「先生，你再不出示簽證跟入境卡的話，我就要請你下車，執行扣留。」另一名邊防人員回道。

瞧，這就是提供過多資訊的壞處。過猶不及。話是沒錯，但你不覺得，資訊是人類的特權，可以盡情享用，不必擔心吸收太多會有壞處？人類之所以能長久繁衍，不正是因為能掌握資訊嗎？

「等等！」我脫口而出，腦袋進入自體防

衛模式，「我手機裡有電子檔！」

幸好我除了有解釋太多的傾向，平時還有囤積東西的好習慣（兩者似乎有共通點），真是謝天謝地。

我施了點科技魔法，透過 Janet 的手機設定 Wi-Fi 熱點，網路斷斷續續的，好不容易找到相關文件，趕緊出示給這兩名焦躁不安的邊防人員看。這下我完全清醒了，寧可乖乖照辦，也不要被扣留在美墨邊境好幾天，害大家老遠開回休士頓幫我拿護照。

一名邊防人員取過我的手機、加州駕照，八成是要對照資料是否相符。我們大家和他靜靜對峙著，另一人員則在不知不覺間回到廂型車後方。

「好了，先生，這樣可以了。」他輕拍車子。「你們可以走了。」

喔耶！

我學到幾個教訓：就算沒跨過美墨國界，只要是靠近國界，也是必須檢查證件的。我一定還漏了什麼。

喔對：千萬別解釋太多。 Ⓖ

Problems with Border Police, and vice-versa

by George

I over explain things. Janet reminds me of this as often as I over explain things, which is frequently. I realise that I'm at this very moment over explaining how I over explain things.

I'm just a fan of giving people as much information as possible. When I was working in a law firm as a trainee solicitor, my emails to clients were packed to the digital gills - turgid with information on the whys and wherefores - and both clients and lawyers alike thought I was giving them too much information about what they wanted to hear.

I should've learnt back then that people want a short and sweet answer to things - even if the question doesn't have a short and sweet answer, but nope I just can't help it: any question that's posed to me acts like a laxative to my brain and out comes the verbal diarrhea. You see I didn't need that verbal diarrhea part - you got the picture much earlier in that sentence – I'm sorry.

And so it was that, during our time in Texas, my over-zealousness in answering questions led to a run in with the law.

It was Christmas Eve, and Janet, the crew and I were en route from Houston to Marfa in our little white van. Before we got into the car, I asked the team whether we'd need our passports, seeing as we were going to be so close to the Mexican border.

"Of course not," came the reply. "We're not leaving the US".

It all sounded reasonable enough, so I left my passport at home. We all get in the van and I promptly fall asleep.

Several hours later, I'm woken up to the sound of US Border Patrol asking for all of our respective passports.

Now, having just woken up from one of those largely uncomfortable multi-hour seated car naps (you know the one: head trying to escape your neck, whilst the rest of your body is suspended by your seatbelt like a stringed puppet on stage), I'm quite rightly in a bit of a daze when la policia come a-knocking.

This is the point where I realise that almost all of the team had their passports with them: largely because the Taiwanese crew's only photo ID were their passports.

Indeed, aside from little old me, Janet was the only one without her passport. But she's an American citizen, with the home state accent and State of Texas ID to match, whilst I'm very much British and at that point still waking up and trying to figure out if we'd actually crossed the border to Mexico.

"Sir can I see your passport please," barked the patrolman (the "please" and the "sir" belied his threatening tone).

"I have this US California licence…"

It could've all ended there, and I would've managed the situation smoothly and succinctly. But I do neither smooth nor succinct and - unfortunately - I wasn't about to start now.

"…but I'm not a US Citizen," I helpfully add, in my slightly-groggy but very much British accent. "Yes - I'm here on a visa."

"Where's your visa, sir?" asked the patrolman, as another emerges from behind our van.

"In my passport," I reply, waking up ever so slightly to the slowly creeping awkwardness of the situation at hand.

"Sir, I'm going to have to ask you to leave the vehicle and be detained here if you can't produce your visa and entry forms", responded the second patrolman.

And that's the problem with providing too much information. Too much of anything is too much, yes, but wouldn't you think that information itself should be something we can all enjoy in an unlimited capacity and not have to worry about suffering any ill-effects? Isn't that how the human race has been so successful thus far in our aggregated lifetime?

"Wait wait!" I blurt out: some sense of self-preservation kicking in within my brain, "I have a digital version on my phone!"

Thank the gods that, along with my propensity to over explain things, comes a seemingly related habit of hoarding.

After some quick technological magic on my part setting up a wifi hotspot with a shoddy connection via Janet's phone to mine, I bring up the relevant papers, and manically display them to the two now very much agitated patrolman. It was very evident from my now wide-awake face that I would prefer not to be held in a cell near the US-Mexico border for however many days it would take for the rest of the team to drive back to Houston to pick up my passport.

One patrolman takes my phone, along with my California driver's licence, presumably to check everything is in order. A small silent standoff ensues with the rest of us and the remaining patrolman. The second patrolman pops back on the other side of the van.

"Alright sir - it all checks out." He taps the van. "Move along please".

Yikes.

Lessons learnt: even if you're not crossing the US-Mexico border, you will be checked if you're near the border. Also - perfect an American accent.

I'm sure I'm forgetting something.

Ah yes: don't over-explain things. Ⓖ

我們從休士頓搭飛機到了 El Paso，從德州東邊跨越一整個德州到達最西邊，花了兩個小時左右。El Paso 離墨西哥很近，眼睛一望過去就是墨西哥國土。我們去的那個區域叫做「Big Bend」，翻作「大彎曲國家公園」，意思就是德州下方那個彎，我們準備在那邊騎馬。George 不會騎馬，這也是他第一次騎馬。一般人第一次騎馬就是繞圈圈慢慢騎，但我們不是，我們是騎山路，而且那裡是沙漠，還有土狼！

我跟 George 的個性很不一樣，我很愛冒險，他卻什麼都擔心！所以一到那邊他就開始問：「有沒有安全帽？」、「有沒有安全帶？」、「馬有沒有更小隻的？」我們跟他說這些馬已經算很小隻了！但他堅決說：「No, No, No 我的腳踩不到地，我要更小隻的！」其實 George 不是膽小，只是他會把所有可能性通通想過一遍，特別是可能發生的「悲劇」，比如可能會跌倒、土狼會跑過來干擾……等等，想很多很多。不過平心而論，那天我們騎了一整天，第一次騎馬就騎整天，還要自己控制馬的所有狀態，已經算是很不錯了。

結果後來 George 騎馬真的全程戴安全帽，而我呢，就是自在享受著騎馬的過程，你會覺得我就像一個牛仔，因為我小時候曾夢想過戴著牛仔帽，很帥氣地騎馬上學，現在好像實現了！

我們在這裡喝到了德州牛仔咖啡，其實它很難喝，只是把咖啡倒進去一大桶熱水，是很淡的黑咖啡。當地人說以前牛仔要帶牛趕路，人很多路途又很遙遠，所以對咖啡的需求量很大，就像平常喝水一樣，不需要太精緻。

那邊有一條溪是德州（美國）與墨西哥的邊界，只要腿一跨過溪就到了墨西哥。那天帶領我們的嚮導 Linda 住在墨西哥，所以每天早上她要到美國工作時經過邊界只要秀一下護照就可以過去，有時甚至只要露臉即可，因為她每天都要來來去去，已經跟當地崗哨很熟了。

雖然「Big Bend」很大不可能到處都設有崗哨，但是當你要離開這區域時還是要接受嚴格檢查。那天我們經過「Big Bend」，開到某個地方突然停下來，邊界警察過來詢問我們從哪裡來。當時整組工作人員都在車上昏睡，一下子沒人知道發生什麼事，被驚醒後大家紛紛拿出護照，我也拿出駕照，只有 George 沒有帶，因為他想我們並不會出國，所以當下整個慌了，一直不斷重複說：「我沒有帶護照、我沒有帶護照」，害那個警察不得不懷疑他是從哪裡來的，還叫 George 下車接受詢問而且不讓我陪同，我們全部工作人員就待在車上乾著急想著該怎麼辦？結果還好 George 的手機裡有護照及簽證照片，很快就沒事了。其實邊界警察只是例行性問一下，卻因為 George 比一般人更容易緊張才發生這個插曲，真是又好氣又好笑。原來這一區叫做 Lajitas，這裡剛好是我姊姊去度蜜月的地方，她跟我說 911 事件發生之前整個邊界管得很鬆，二十幾年前他們的蜜月旅行在德州，但中間有天晚上睡在墨西哥，隔一天再回到德州，但當時進出都不用檢查護照！可見 911 影響之大，今非昔比。

Chapter. 02

夢想進化論
Evolution of a Dream

童年時期的夢想，
與夢想的愛情！

以前我曾經夢想要成為一個小提琴家，也曾經想當醫生，但現在我做的事情也是我的夢想實現。自己一個人要成就夢想其實很容易，家人總是毫無保留地支持我，我要想的事情只有自己與世界的關係而已，但如果要兩個人一起實現夢想，要考慮的事情是很多很多的；但是，我始終相信這並不表示兩個人在一起就會犧牲什麼、妥協什麼。雖然要考慮的事情很多，但是多了一個人在身邊陪你，因此並不是把時間、思考、力氣「分」出去給另一個人，而是邀請一個人「一起」了解這個世界！

我曾經交了一個法國男朋友，他具備了各種條件，大概是 George 之前最可能結婚的對象吧！當時我覺得可以為他放棄工作，與他在法國一起生活。後來我們還是分手啦，而分手之後我來到台灣，有了現

在的工作。當我回頭看那段關係，才發現那樣的狀態根本不是我自己的樣子，有事業與沒事業的我，差異真的非常大。有工作的我是有自信的，不需要誰來填補我的生活的空缺，對我而言這樣的愛情才是真正看見彼此，兩個人在人生的道路上一起走，而不是要求另一個人來成就自己要走的那條道路，這樣是很不公平的吧！

夢想的挫敗是禮物

從小到大難免遭遇過大大小小的挫折（這就是人生嘛），小時候最印象深刻的大挫折，是跟小提琴有關的。我曾經為了一個小提琴比賽，勤練一首曲子達一年，就為了贏得這個一年一度的比賽，取得與大團演出的資格。到了比賽當天，我自信滿滿地來到會場，準備好自己的樂譜、譜架。不料，臨上台之際，主辦單位告知我上台不可以看譜。

他們討論後決定給我時間再練一遍。其實我勤練這一年多以來早就熟記這個曲子了，而臨上台前那次多出來的不看譜練習，是我從開始練起拉得最美好的一次。於是我自信滿滿地上台了。演出一開始，都非常順利，但是過沒多久，我突然停住了。我的腦海裡一片空白，所有關於這首曲子的一切都在那一刻被抽空了；對於這突如其來的停頓，我的伴奏也不知如何繼續演奏，於是他也停下來。舞台凝結在那裡，整間演奏廳都靜默了。

我收起自己的震驚，強裝鎮定走到伴奏身旁，指指樂譜示意「我們從這裡再開始吧。」但同樣的事又再次發生了。後來我並沒有拉完，評審請我下台，每一位評審講評的時候都很客氣地說我拉得很好，只有跟我最熟識的那位評審，輪到他講評時，他只說了一句：「Janet，你怎麼了？」聽到這句話我眼淚撲簌簌掉個不停，一句話也答不出來。小時候小提琴就是我的夢

想、我的一切，這個經驗給我的打擊是無法計量的，至今我還是極度害怕背東西，無論是樂譜還是台詞等等。

但是，這個經驗給我了另一個禮物，那就是讓我參加了姐姐的畢業典禮，因為當時樂團的演出會與姐姐的畢業典禮時間衝個正著，我若取得演出機會，我們全家當天就必需分批去不同地方，而因為落選，我們全家得以一起參加我姐姐的畢業典禮。而這個挫敗經驗之所以讓我記一輩子，是因為它是相當豐富飽滿的，不是只有挫敗，而是最後得到了祝福，我也在祝福中明白，所有的挫敗、痛苦都是有理由的，而如果能夠避免一直困在因挫敗而生的負面情緒裡，而是能夠將這個經驗放到更長的時間裡面來看，就會等到讓挫敗經驗轉變為能量的那一刻！

兩個人夢想進化論

當我們決定一起踏上婚姻的旅途之後，我發現自己憧憬的生活樣貌，有了一些轉變。有了事業的我，過去幾年一直是不顧一切往前衝，無論要去哪都很有動力，從不瞻前顧後；以前我始終是一個無法靜下來的人，偶爾靜靜地待在同一個地方是可以的，但這樣的例子比較少，大部份的時候我很難接受到了一個地方卻哪裡也不去，始終嚮往著探索與冒險，巨大的生活變動都能欣然接受；過去我只要一靜下來，就會湧出焦慮，深怕自己錯過了什麼、少做了什麼，我有好多好多想做的事！

現在，我卻能停下來享受與家人在一起的、身邊很日常的小小樂趣，我可以陪我的姪子在家玩上個三天足不出戶，我很享受與家人一起的晨間運動時間……。我還是個很有衝勁的人，還是那個永遠都準備好要啟程的我，但是現在可以在動與靜之間調適，除了充滿變動的能量之外，也可以在安靜中閒適。

生命中的轉變，
將兩個人帶往更長的路上

我跟 George 認識的時候才二十四、五歲左右；跟現在相比起來，那個時候的我們，都跟現在很不一樣。十年前的我並不清楚自己的方向，有些迷失，加上當時我因為當模特兒而厭食。對於男人、對於感情，我是非常依賴的，好像可以為感情放棄我自己的工作與夢想，不顧一切與對方在一起。而那個時候的 George，是個自信心過剩的人，看似非常有自信，做什麼都可以成功，感情也是，追求女性無往不利；這樣的 George 雖然做什麼都看似輕而易舉，但是實際上人生也沒有太多方向。他常常笑說，以前他發誓不要跟華人也不要跟希臘人交往，因為不想找跟他長得像的人當戀人甚至是妻子，結果結婚的對象就是個華人。

所以，如果當時我們就談戀愛，我們的關係一定是分手收場的吧，我一定會極度依賴他，他一定會嫌我太黏人而厭煩，而他若拋棄我，以當時我的狀況來看，應該會日日以淚洗面長達一年時間吧哈哈！

而這十年之間，我們經歷的所有的事情，已經把我們各自琢磨成更趨近彼此的人。這十年之間我經歷過靠自己爬起來的日子，放下了很多事之後，我終於不需要再為了別人目光而與自己真實的聲音對抗。而他的演員生涯並非總是一帆風順，當演員並非一般想像那麼光鮮亮麗，要成為能夠站在眾人面前的演員，不是一件容易的事，他經歷過那些不知所措，而變得更謙遜。

兩個人一起的夢想進化

Ⓖ 我生涯最大的挑戰之一，就是放棄法律事業，將自己的跑道全部移轉到演藝事業。我跟 Janet 兩個人都一樣，家族裡沒有任何成員是這個行業的人，因此沒有任何先例可以遵循，並且雙方家裡原本的期待，都是我們各自都能做個「嚴肅」的行業，Janet 是從醫，我這方面則是法律。所以我們兩個人算是跳進了一個未知的領域，而未來到底會不會走得順利，以後慢慢就會知道答案了。小時候我也想像長大的自己會結婚，以前幻想擇偶條件好像就蠻成熟的——希望未來伴侶是有自信、有個性的人，也要風趣，更重要的是，她會因為我的笑話而笑。

Ⓙ 看來你妻子的個性並沒有離你以前幻想的太遠喔！

Ⓖ 小時候老師叫我們寫未來自傳的時候，我寫自己是個獨角喜劇演員，會結婚，太太名叫 Sarah……。

Ⓙ 喔！所以職業跟太太的名字錯了，但好歹婚姻的部份對了。

Ⓖ 婚姻這件事確確實實改變了生命。結婚之前，我歷經自信的兩個階段，二十幾歲時的自信是未經雕琢的，是毫不瞻前顧後的自信，回頭過來看，才明白那樣的自信置換了青春的不安全感。到了三十幾歲的時候，自信源自於對自我的瞭解與發現，這時候的自信是更細緻的。而結婚之後，才真正開啟了第三個階段的自信心，此時的自信是成熟的，也是穩定的，我還不太能細緻地描述，但是我確切知道這是只有與對的人結為連理才會得到的自信。到了今天，我深刻地感受到自己是多麼幸運的人。我很幸運能夠照著自己最喜歡的路徑走，做自己真正喜歡的事，跟小時候自己的未來自傳一樣，在演藝事業發展。更幸運的是找到一個我愛的人，而她剛好也愛我。我實在不敢貪婪地索討更多了，不然老天爺大概會狠狠賞我一巴掌吧！

Big Bend 國家公園（大彎曲國家公園）的
面積是台灣的三倍大，裡面充滿沙漠與水
融合而成的地貌，並且橫跨德州跟墨西
哥。我們在那裡找了一位當地人 Charlie
帶我們划獨木舟。因為那條河是德州與墨
西哥的邊界之一，整個划的過程會一下在
德州一下在墨西哥，George 就開玩笑說：
「糟糕！這樣我的漫遊費會很貴喔！」。
而且因為他沒去過墨西哥，所以硬要我划
過去墨西哥那邊，還比了個到此一遊的動
作：「我到了墨西哥囉！」

Dec.
27

「Terlingua」這個地名來自西班牙文「Tres Lenguas」「三種語言」之意，因為當地匯集了英文、西班牙文、原住民語三種語言。

Terlingua 本來是一個非常熱鬧的地方，因為那裡曾經發現過貴金屬，是一個淘金城市，但當淘金熱潮過了之後人潮漸漸散去，逐漸變成一個鬼城，之後才開始有藝術家、音樂家搬進來，稍微復興了這個城市，是很獨特、可愛的地方。

在 Terlingua 我們認識兩位鄉村音樂家一起做即興演出。其實在場許多人都會一種樂器，像是有人帶著一大盒口琴在那邊炫技、有人帶著復古吉他……我的小提琴則是一把很輕的碳纖維小提琴，是我特別為了這個行程買下的，因為一般木頭材質小提琴很怕極端的氣候，但我這把不怕熱也不怕冰，超適合這次橫跨四季、溫度極端的旅程。

我們一個一個加入即興演奏，大家一邊玩一邊唱一邊跳，超 high 的！他們有人玩一種超級大的呼拉圈，我們一邊演奏樂器他們一邊搖，讓我想到德州一句俗語說：「Everything is bigger in Texas!」，連 George 看到也嘖嘖稱奇！

Lajitas 的市長是一頭羊！我記得有一年沒有人想當市長，就推派一頭羊出來當，至今這頭羊已經當了三輪市長。牠很愛喝啤酒跟吃墨西哥捲餅，我們突發奇想，如果為了拍片必須討好「市長」，就餵牠吃喜歡的東西，然後把食物放在牠面前問：「我們可以進去這裡拍嗎？」接著上下晃動食物，牠一定會跟著上下點頭，這時我們就當作是市長允許囉！

這次旅程顛覆了許多工作人員對德州的印象。一般人看到沙漠會覺得很熱,但其實它很冷,我們剛抵達的時候地上還有雪呢!其實德州很大,跟法國一樣大,它有海邊、有可以滑雪的高山、還有沙漠、平地和城市,非常豐富!

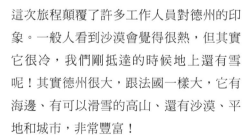

Marfa 是一個藝術城市，我住德州的時候完全沒有聽過這裡，後來 Prada 在 Marfa 公路某個不知名的地點，設置了一個裝置藝術店鋪，Beyoncé 在那拍了一張很有名的照片，才把這個裝置藝術點還有 Marfa 炒紅了。

這間飯店 The Hotel Paisano 也是一九五六年的電影《巨人》拍攝場景，由伊莉莎白・泰勒、洛・赫遜和詹姆斯・狄恩主演。

事情
沒有這麼容易

by George

我老是聽大家對 Janet 說，她擁有世上最棒的工作，能趁機環遊世界，談談所見所聞和邂逅際遇——還可以賺錢。

就讓我來告訴你們吧：事情沒有看起來這麼容易。

首先，你可能會非常非常累。搞不好凌晨四點就得起床（或被迫睜開眼睛），早餐以便利商店買的雞蛋三明治果腹，跟同樣昏昏沉沉的工作人員塞在廂型車裡，匆忙化妝。車子疾駛，今天有十個點要跑，原本前往第一站車程要三小時，現在必須縮短為二個半，否則傍晚來不及拍美輪美奐的夕陽。

接下來十五小時的拍攝期間，你必須保持頭腦清醒、容光煥發、心情愉悅，縱使腳痠、頭痛、背疼、人不舒服，也由不得你：攝影機前，你就得開開心心的。

經過五十天左右、馬不停蹄主持旅遊節目，終於可以體會 Janet 的心情，容我斬釘截鐵的說：我還是比較喜歡當演員。演戲時，不論在舞台或攝影棚，你可以偽裝為另一個角色。不必一天到晚強顏歡笑（除非角色本來就是那樣）。起碼演戲時（演舞台劇可能就沒這麼好了），你還有休息時間，可以躲進多半有開空調的拖車或休息室。

或許，這也是為什麼，旅遊節目中我們特別增設的串場戲劇橋段，我尤其樂在其中。

有串場戲劇橋段的旅遊節目並不多見，但導演是希望，既然這系列已頗具實驗性，不如就再讓它錦上添花。我恭敬不如從命：依據旅程內容，為大家構思或多或少相關的概略腳本。

不必當自己，即使只有短短一下子，也是

很棒的一件事！（起碼暫時脫離旅遊節目主持人的身分，否則要面對各種任務、考驗、險徑，害我老是緊張兮兮）。暫且不必對攝影機說話，不必即興發揮，來個一語驚人，娛樂觀眾或配合主持搭檔了。我大可唸大字報（身為編劇，當然要把字寫很大了），盡情表達憤怒、焦躁或失望，只有一下也好！（換成旅遊節目，這樣可是犯了大忌）。

我也不曉得 Janet 是怎麼辦到的，主持旅遊節目才不是世上最棒的工作，應該說，對她而言，那是最棒的工作。她對每件事都有源源不絕的熱情，語言能力一級棒（隨便點一種語言，她八成都會），幾乎跟什麼人都能相處。再者，她很堅強。想當旅遊節目主持人，你必須非常堅強，要能堅毅不拔、忍受痛楚：首先是身體上的痛楚，譬如腳疼、背痛、身體不舒服、頭疼；再來是情緒上的痛楚，你得忍耐煩人又惜字如金的主持搭檔（譬如我）。

或許你有 Janet 的特質。如果這樣，快來上旅遊節目吧，但願我不在場，否則你就要聽我碎碎念，抱怨腿痠或好累之類的。ⓒ

It's all about the Drama

by George

I keep hearing people tell Janet that she has the best job in the world; how great it is that she gets to travel all over the place, and talk about all the things she sees and the people she meets - all for a living.

I'm here to tell you: it's not as easy as it looks.

First off - you can be very very tired. You might have woken up (or forced to open your eyes at least) at 4am, consume a convenience-store-bought egg sandwich for breakfast whilst simultaneously doing your makeup in a van full of equally groggy crew members, whilst all of you hurtle towards the first of ten destinations via a three hour drive that you have complete in two and a half as you want to film that amazing sunrise.

You then have to be of sound enough mind and bright and cheerful for the next fifteen hours of filming, and there's no room for sore feet or headaches or tired backs or general uncomfortableness: it's happy happy all the way for the cameras.

After fifty or so non-stop days of living in Janet's shoes as a travel show host, I can safely say that I much prefer acting. When acting - on stage or on set - you can hide in another character. You don't need to be happy happy enthusiastic-y all the time (unless the character is that way inclined). When filming at least (not so much in theatre), you can take breaks and retreat to what is usually a nice air-conditioned trailer or greenroom.

That's probably why I very much enjoyed the drama segments that we filmed in between the travel show stuff.

It's obviously not usual to film drama segments for a travel show, but Tim the director wanted to mix it up a bit with this already quite experimental series, and I was happy to oblige: coming up with scripts for bits we could do that had some vague connection to the travel segments.

And what a joy it was to not be me for a moment! (Or at least not to be the travel show version of me, who gets genuinely anxious about every task, trial or trail that we needed to embark upon). I could avoid talking directly to the camera for a while, and read lines from a script (a great script obviously seeing as

I was the scriptwriter), as opposed to having to come up with something clever for the audience or co-host on the spot. And be angry or agitated or disappointed for a while! (Three moods that are generally forbidden from travel shows).

I don't know how Janet does it - being a travel show host is not the best job in the world: it's the best job for her. Because she has an almost unending enthusiasm for everything, she is a great communicator (name a language and there's a chance she can speak it), and can get on with almost everyone. And she's tough - you need to be tough to be a travel show host; you need to have endurance and a tolerance for pain: physical pain from your feet to your back to your body and your head, and emotional pain from annoying or reticent co-hosts (such as me for example).

Perhaps you have the same qualities that Janet possesses. If so - get yourself on a travel show, and hope that you don't have me there to complain about my sore legs or how tired I am. Ⓖ

George Young

德州有個知名的節慶：休士頓牛仔節，我小時候每年都會參加，裡面的比賽有「牛仔競技」（Rodeo）、「騎牛」（Bull Riding）……等等。Bull Riding 就是你坐上公牛，以單手抓住牛的套繩、另一手舉起來，任牠跳跳跳，努力不要被甩出去。我小時候就是看這個比賽讓我很想當牛仔，因為覺得牛仔們看起來好帥！這個比賽只有六秒，為了這六秒你要準備一整年，六秒一結束若沒有晉級，這一年就形同結束。所以你可以想像那個訓練過程

還有比賽壓力有多大。我過去以為他們的工作有很多玩的成份、或有很多次比賽機會，結果根本不是這樣。

在節慶裡還有「休士頓家畜展」（Livestock Show），牛仔養自己的動物，牛羊雞豬什麼都有，每年比看誰養的動物最棒，學生為了把動物養到最好，會花很多錢和時間去養，第一名可以得到幾萬塊美金。還記得我姐姐也有參加過，她還拿牛奶去洗動物的皮膚呢！

休士頓牛仔節裡的「女子馬術障礙賽」是比速度，賽場中設有三個障礙點，騎士騎在馬上繞完三個點一圈回到原點。在馬上你的腳要一直夾馬的身體，還要配合牠的節奏，控制牠走、繞圈……真的沒有想像中簡單。一般繞完一次的時間是 36 秒，我想如果我繞完一圈的秒數是他們的雙倍，應該也算不錯的成績。我試了一次，差不多是雙倍再多一點點的秒數。George

雖然沒什麼騎馬經驗，但他說他也要比，我調侃他說：「你確定嗎？？」沒想到他竟然用跑的把路線跑完，還比我快，哈哈！

我騎馬跟喝酒一樣，很有膽子，但我並沒有什麼技術或策略，總之一上馬就想：「Ok, let's go!」因此我的騎馬姿勢應該不太正確，反正不要被甩下去就好了。

我們雖然沒有參與 Rodeo，但卻跟牛仔們
去接受訓練。我覺得牛仔就像運動員，野
外放牧的牛仔，牛走失時要很俐落地騎在
馬上用繩子把牛套回來。他們也要好好照
顧自己的馬，畢竟馬就像是這些運動員的
裝備，一旦受傷就無法比賽。我們看到現
場有幾個小牛仔，他們是老闆的小孩，小
小年紀騎馬、上牛都很熟練，從小就受到
很好的訓練。

我們上公牛的時候可以感覺牠劇烈的呼吸，隨時都蓄勢待發，只要一開門就會衝出去。這其實是非常危險的動作，如果沒有跟著公牛律動，隨時都有可能會飛出去！但如果不幸飛出去也有方法：為了防止牛踢你，掉下去時一定要趕快滾走，以防止牛又跑過來。

教練示範完後我們故意捉弄 George：「嘿！George 換你了！」可以想見，以George 這麼容易緊張的人一定連忙說：「Oh……No！No！No！」看他害怕地用祈求眼神看著導演說：「導演，這裡要拍嗎？」導演說：「喔……要啊……」結

果 George 就更緊張了，我們還假裝在旁邊安撫他：「別擔心我們只是要讓你體會一下在牛上的感覺，沒有要你真的試。」

柵欄上有一個門的卡榫，當它打開時會發出「卡卡」的聲音，門便會跟著打開，通常牛聽到聲音、看到門打開就會衝出去。所以當 George 坐上牛之後，教練故意弄了一下那個卡榫，當下 George 以為牛會衝出去，嚇得「花容失色」，他事後說他差點尿出來！老實說如果是我被騙我也會嚇死，因為那頭牛聽到卡榫的聲音真的有被驚動到的感覺，害 George 被嚇壞了。

在德州我們騎了好多次馬,曾經騎過山路,也騎過 Rodeo,而這次是真的在趕牛!德州的牛叫做「long horn」,牠的角特別長,也很兇,跟 Rodeo 馬訓練的方式很不一樣。Rodeo 的馬要一直鼓勵牠,屬於表演性質,但這邊的馬卻不能讓牠受到驚嚇,因為馬一跑起來就有危險性,要帶著牠一步一步慢慢走,如果感覺牠有受到驚嚇,就要趕緊安撫牠。很多牛仔因為馬驚動了牛一起衝出去,牛仔失去重心掉下去死掉,因此要特別小心。此外也要注意不讓牛跑起來,因為這樣牛比較容易骨折或受傷,也會減少脂肪量。一開始牧場老闆很謹慎,問我們有沒有騎過,很怕我們會出事,因為當牛近距離看人,或者要聚集牠們的時候,牠們張大眼看著你時都要非常穩定。

為了體驗馬跟牛之間的關係,我們將牛趕到另一邊去,我們使用的套索(lasso)可以精準套中很遠的牛,將牠拉過來。就這樣我們慢慢將散開的牛集中起來,這時才體驗到牛仔真正的工作,這裡的牛仔跟 Rodeo 牛仔的帥氣真的不一樣!而這邊的牛仔也是隨手一杯咖啡,隨時幫自己取暖跟提神。

騎完之後最開心的亮點是食物！我們跟著德州牛仔吃他們平常吃的食物，早餐跟晚餐都非常豐富，晚餐有各式牛肉食品，比如牛排、牛筋、牛香腸，另外還有豬肋排、豆子、米飯……通通都是他們自己煮的，還有自己烤的麵包、甜點還有南瓜派、蘋果派……。別以為騎馬看起來沒有在動，但騎完之後會非常非常餓，不知是因為全身緊繃還是怎樣，就是會想吃很多。果然如牛仔們所說，一天最開心的時刻就是回家喝酒、吃飯的時光。

那天我的爸爸媽媽也開車過來，一起玩 Uno 還有其他遊戲，過了很特別的跨年。雖然我們十點就睡了，也沒有像在台北一樣去 101 倒數、看煙火，但這對從小在倫敦成長的都市小孩 George 來說，是很不一樣的體驗。

Chapter. 03

看見彼此的記憶
He said; She said

關係的轉變

我們十年前就認識了，過去十年來我們一直沒有火花，也許彼此有好感，但還不至於會相戀，所謂「朋友以上，戀人未滿」大概就是這個狀態。直到有一天他生病了，在照顧他的過程裡，我心想喔我的天啊我想要照顧這個人！後來我們才表述了彼此的心意，經過這麼多年後，終於在一起了。其實剛開始在一起的時候我們想的是過一天算一天，我們兩個分開的時間比在一起還要長，交往的話說不定一下子就結束了；過了一個禮拜我們感情越來越好，相處起來非常快樂，而過了一個月之後……我心裡就非常清楚，如果可以，我想要跟他在一起一輩子！

所以人與人之間的關係，不是看一時的，而是看長久的，時間長了就會有答案，說不定我們現在結婚了也不是最後的答案。

第一個共同記憶

Ⓙ 我們相識過程的實情，一直有一個地方是我們的討論的爭議點……

Ⓖ 到底我們是先見過面才第一次通電話，還是通過電話後才見面呢……？

Ⓙ 我們第一個共同的記憶，結果兩個人記得的內容居然就有落差哈哈！其實沒有什麼好爭的啦，反正我們現在都結婚了，只是我們還是常常在講這件事！我們認識過程是當時我的模特兒經紀公司說有一個殺青酒，想介紹男生給我，問我要不要去。當時有兩個混血男生，一個是醫生，一個是律師，律師就是 George，但是經紀公司的人原本要把那位叫 Ian 的醫生介紹給我，因為當年我也讀醫科，但是我跟 George 就先在 Ian 去上廁所期間先認識了哈哈！我記得很清楚當時 George 在打撞球，我跟他聊得很開心，完全把 Ian 這個

人拋在腦後了。後來我們常講電話聊得很開心。

Ⓖ 這裡就是我們的爭議點了。到底是先講電話才認識，還是先認識才講電話呢？我真的記得我們是先講電話才認識的。

Ⓙ 但我覺得不合理耶。

Ⓖ （聳肩）

Ⓙ 那天我感冒有點不舒服，吃了藥又跟人喝了一點，還抽水煙……總之當時的情境非常戲劇性，我眼睛盯著 George……就昏倒了！而且 George 還沒接住我！

Ⓖ 我有。

Ⓙ 才沒有，我醒來頭上腫了一個大包。

Ⓖ 那一定是之後的事，我不知道那個腫包哪裡來的。

Ⓙ 背後也有喔！

Ⓖ 我絕對有接住你……

Ⓙ 哈哈！總之那天起我們就成了無話不聊的朋友。當時我們兩個對彼此都沒有談戀愛的那種幻想，就這樣過了十年，期間不斷有女性朋友會問我：「Janet 你這位朋友是誰啊？他很帥耶！」我才慢慢意識到他有一些魅力。

Ⓖ 我們當朋友當了這麼長時間才在一起，實際上真的是個性天差地遠，基本上是相反的。不過我們之間會依照當時的情緒與情境達到平衡，這跟手足之間的關係很像，有時一方是壞心情，另一方就把好心情更端出來一點。我們之間也有那種可以映照出彼此的動力。

互補的性格

我跟 George 都是很獨立的人，就算在一起之後，這點也始終不變。我們各自在地球的不同角落有事業，兩個人就像平行線一樣。獨立的人當然有走在一起的可能，但朋友說我們常常好像一個不小心，兩條線就走遠了，要記得拉回來一下啊。所以我們也會盡可能安排飛去陪對方的時間。這確實不容易，我們兩個「世界空中飛人」經常到處工作（即便 George 說他不喜歡旅行哈哈），而我們每次去工作就是百分之百地投入，工作一結束就在心裡把一切都打包好，預備下一次的旅程。像我們這麼能夠收拾自己的獨立之人，實在是很難相聚。

而這次難得在一起的旅程很有趣，使我們更加看清楚彼此的差異；雖然早就知道我們多麼不同，但一起的旅程讓我們更加地明白，正是因為這麼天差地遠的差異，才讓我們有機會看得更清楚那些將我們緊緊牽動在一起的是什麼。就像 George 說的，我們之間存在著可以映照出彼此的動力。George 也說，我們是同樣事情的不同面向：我們之間既相異，也相同，這就像我們吃飯的觀念一模一樣，我們常常喜歡吃一模一樣的東西，但就算吃不一樣的食物，我們就會分給對方吃，這樣都可以嘗到了。

這些我們兩個既相同也不同的地方，完全可以體現在旅行——對於旅行，我們兩個的欲望跟想法實在是太天差地遠了！我很愛冒險，George 喜歡靜靜地待在一個地方，兩個人完全相反。這次南極的旅途中 George 曾說道，如果不是我，他就不會有這麼多動力去探索與冒險；他嘴巴上都會唸說這個很危險，心裡嘀咕著：「其實我也不是這麼愛到處冒險……」，最後終究還是跟著到處跑。而我，雖然熱愛冒險，最喜歡去別人不曾到過的地方，但是我也很喜歡靜下來陪伴他躺著，一起做個日光浴也好、一起讀書也好。我還記得有一次我們一起去東加，他提議來做個日光浴吧！我也一口答應，曬著曬著……我就安靜地睡著了。

我們就是這樣，在差異中又對彼此有很多的關照與好奇，這是我們共同的價值，也是把我們倆牽起來的方式；一旦確認了彼此的價值觀是不相悖的，那兩個人的關係就可以很簡單，可以一起做的事情就會有很多的不同的空間與可能！

從另一半的眼中看見自己

Ⓙ 認識 George 之後我一直想更進步！我始終覺得他比我風趣、比我聰明，大家都非常喜歡他。他的反應很快，文筆非常好……總之他很多事情都很好就對了啦！他一直讓我有一種想要進步的動力。

Ⓖ 我也有這種感覺，就是覺得 Janet 讓我變成了一個更好的人，尤其是一個更果決一點的人。從以前到現在我始終是個不太擅長做決定的人，無論是決定要穿什麼衣服，或者是跟事業有關的抉擇，對我而言做決定始終不是件簡單的事。但是我從 Janet 的行動力中學到了一件很重要的事——做決定並不要命啊。而且，其實真正要命的事情才是該擔心的……。

Ⓙ 等等我還沒誇獎完你呢。George 有兩個弟弟有自閉症，他因此對自閉症有很多了解，也對自閉症者的任何事都有很大的參與的熱忱；每個人多少都有一些自己關心的議題，我也一樣，但我從來沒有像他對自閉症者的事情這樣付出。我也很喜歡他的自信。其實我不是個那麼有自信的人，但是既然他這麼有自信、又聰明、又對某些事物如此投入，而且任何事都能做得很好，這麼美好的人，最後卻選擇了我……這麼說來，我一定也很不錯！

Ⓖ Janet 真的是一個很平易近人的人，可以輕易地與人們打交道。我就無法一直保持這種狀態，心情對的話可以，但無法像 Janet 這樣持續不斷地對人產生好奇，也願意讓人親近。我們一起工作兼旅行的這五十天裡，我親身感受到 Janet 對所有人事物的熱情，如果沒有親眼目睹，是不會相信天底下有這般熱忱的！

關於昏倒事件，
她是這麼說的……

by Janet

我們以前都很常跟朋友出去玩。那年二〇〇四，我們都還是青春學子，無憂無慮，又沒有工作壓力，何不呢？George 剛來台北，師大語言中心的同學邀我去一間新開的酒吧／夜店／騷莎音樂酒館，我就邀他一起去了。想說，這位新認識的朋友看來傻呼呼的，我朋友應該會喜歡。當時，我才跟前男友分手，George 對我來說，就是一位風趣幽默的英國男孩，這幾個禮拜剛好來台北，所以我並沒有多想。

到了夜店，我同學立刻對 George 投以飢渴的目光，然後對我眨眨眼，又推了推我。實在不曉得他們在想什麼。我對他又沒特別感覺。老實說，我覺得他可能是同性戀，所以從沒往那方面去想。也不知道是什麼「奇怪」原因，我朋友都覺得他超級無敵可愛，還問他是否單身。

那晚我們聊天跳舞，玩得很開心。還記得因為受涼，身體不太舒服，特地事前吃了感冒藥。藥應該有效，當晚到了夜店，我突然渾身帶勁，搖擺身體、談天說笑，十分盡興。有人邀我們試試「呼卡」（即「水煙」，起源於波斯，很快就紅遍中東。以水過濾菸草的煙）。我不抽菸的，換成平時，我一定會婉拒，但當時我根本不知道呼卡是什麼，有人說那是蘋果口味的菸，我於是就屈服於好奇心了。

結果，沒想到我這麼會抽。照他們指示吸進一大口煙，含在嘴裡，但我一定有點含太久了，吐出口時，感到一陣天旋地轉，頭暈目眩。

為了耍帥，我輕輕起身，假裝若無其事。菸草加上感冒藥，效果一定太強了，只記得自己下一秒，轉身對 George 說：「我需要坐下。」緊接著就昏了過去。

我真的昏厥過去。

忘了自己是怎麼昏過去的，只清楚記得有跟George說，我需要坐下。

漸漸醒來，音樂在耳畔響起，差點就要叫我姊把鬧鐘收音機給關了。以為自己身在休士頓老家，吵死人的音樂不停從我姊收音機流瀉出來，偏偏該起床上學的我，還想賴床五分鐘。

感覺音樂漸漸大聲，這才意會到自己不在家，而那也不是我姊的鬧鐘。想動動手臂，卻動彈不得。死魚一般黏在身上。慢慢的，發現自己是坐著，頭靠在某種軟軟的東西上。現實狀況有如一面快速移動的牆（倘若牆會移動），硬生生朝我直撲而來。

突然意識到自己身在何處，感覺是靠在某人身上——而且是男人。我坐在夜店躺椅上，四周人跳得渾然忘我，唯獨我想動都動不了。剛從昏迷中醒來，疲憊睏倦，四肢毫無反應。

首先能動的是頭，卻又不想動，就怕要面對現實。剛剛發生的一切，令人尷尬到不知所措。我這輩子從沒在酒吧或夜店昏倒。人家會怎麼看我？八成會想，我一定是喝太多，不然就是不懂拿捏底線，才會喝到掛。他們定會覺得我是個吊兒郎當的人。還會一輩子取笑我。他們一定會……喔我的老天。頭還是別抬得好。說不定只要我繼續坐在那，等派對結束，眾人呈鳥獸散，我就不必面對現實了。

然而，派對愈夜愈熱鬧，酒吧絲毫沒歇息的跡象。看來，就算想逃避現實，也由不得我了。緩緩抬起全身唯一聽從大腦指令的部位，仰起臉，往上一看。

只見 George 俯視著我，臉上露出一抹淡淡的微笑。起碼乍看是微笑。他手裡似乎拿著一罐啤酒。無論如何，一句話忍不住逬出口中：「你真可愛。」

該死。我腦袋一定秀逗了。怎麼不快喚醒雙腿，只顧著害我講些不得體的話？好吧，所幸腦子轉得快，立刻想到如何接話，以逃脫窘境。我說，很抱歉昏倒了，我不曾這樣的，不曉得怎會發生這種事。八成是水煙被人下藥了。千錯萬錯都不是我的錯。

George 只回了一句：「喔，妳有昏倒喔？我都沒發現，還以為妳在跳一種很炫的舞步。」喔，他真的好可愛。真想帶他回家，陪我一輩子。

不過，好事多磨，就像童話或所有精采絕倫的故事一樣，免不了要幾番輾轉波折，才能如願以償。

你或許好奇，關於昏倒事件，我／他到底想說什麼？總算起身，正打算一笑置之，我揉揉手臂，赫然發現手肘跟頭都腫了一大包，疼痛不已。

音樂小聲點！等一下……這代表，我有撞到桌子，或甚至倒在地上。也就是說，我昏倒的時候，覺得 George 好可愛的念頭立刻一掃而空，現在我只怪他沒扶我。他不是個男人嗎？竟然連扶我一下都不肯，忍心看我倒下去，頭跟手肘猛然撞到某樣東西。

喏，罪證確鑿。這身瘀青，足以證明「某人」並非我的救命恩人，竟可眼睜睜看我這落難女子飽受瘀青摧殘。所以說，我當然要讓 George 等個幾年，才肯再度被他迷個神魂顛倒囉。①

Our first night out - she said...

by Janet

We used to go out a lot with our friends. It was 2004, we were young, carefree, pretty much unemployed students at the time, so why not? George was still relatively new in town so when my classmates from the Mandarin Training Center at National Taiwan Normal University decided to check out a new bar/club/salsa lounge, I invited him to come. I thought my friends would like my new goofy friend. I was still just getting over a heartbreak, so I didn't really see George in any other way than as a really fun and funny guy from England who happened to be in town for a few weeks.

When we arrived, my classmates immediately gave George the hungry eye look and the wink wink, nudge nudge to me. I didn't know what they were talking about. I absolutely did not see George in that way.n fact, I thought he might have been gay, so I really dismissed any idea of being attracted to him. But for some *strange* reason, all of my friends thought he was SUPER DUPER cute and asked if he was single.

We had a great time dancing and hanging out that night. I remember being a little bit sick with a cold so I was on some cold medicine. I guess the cold medicine was working its magic by the time we got to the club because I was suddenly full of energy, dancing, laughing, having a ball. We were invited to try hookah for the first time. (Hookah, is water pipe which originated from Persia and quickly spread throughout the Middle East -t uses water to filter the the tobacco smoke.) I don't smoke, so I normally would have declined, but I had no idea what hookah was at the time and somebody mentioned something about apple flavored smoke and so curiosity got the best of me.

Turns out, I'm really good at inhaling smoke. I took a huge puff of smoke and held it like they told me to. I must have held it a bit too long because by the time I exhaled it, the world was spinning and I felt so light-headed.

But trying to be cool, I casually stood up, pretending that I was totally fine. The tobacco combined with my cold medicine must have really done a number on me because the next second, all I remember is turning around to tell George "I need to sit down." and then promptly passing out.

I fainted.

I don't actually remember the act of fainting of course. But I distinctly remember telling George that I needed to sit down.

When I first started to come to, I heard music, and I wanted to tell my sister to turn off her annoying alarm. I thought I was back at home in Houston and my sister's radio alarm was blasting annoying music while I was trying to sleep that extra 5 minutes before having to get ready for school.

As I slowly heard the music louder and louder, I realized that I wasn't at home and that wasn't my sister's alarm. I tried moving my arms and I couldn't. They were dead weight next to my body. Then, I gathered that I was sitting up and my head was leaning against something soft. The reality of the situation hit me quickly, like a fast moving wall (if walls could move).

I suddenly realized where I was and it dawned on me that I was leaning on somebody - a guy - while sitting on a lounge chair in the middle of the club where people were still dancing like there was no tomorrow, and I simply couldn't move my body. It was still in a post-faint stupor and my limbs were not responding.

The first thing that I could actually move was my head, but I didn't want to move it because that would mean that I had to face the reality of the situation. And I was so embarrassed of what had just happened. Never in my life have I ever fainted while in a bar or club. What were people going to think of me? They were going to think that I had over drank or didn't know my limit and fainted from too much alcohol. They were going to think I was so irresponsible. They were going to make fun of me forever. They were going to…oh god. I didn't want to lift up my head. Maybe if I just sat here long enough, the party would end and everybody would go home and then I wouldn't have to "face the music."

But the party was going strong and the bar wasn't going to be closing any time soon. I was going to have to face the salsa music, like it or not. I slowly lifted the only part of my body that was responding to my brain's commands, and I lifted up my head to look up.

What I saw was George looking down at me with a little grin on his face. Or at least I think it was a grin on his face. I think he may have had a beer in his hand still. Either way, the words came out of my mouth before I could stop them. I said "you're cute."

Damnit. Stupid brain. Why didn't it work on fixing my legs rather than spewing out random words from my mouth? At least it was quick to try and get out of the situation. I proceeded to apologize for fainting, trying to explain over and over again that this has never happened to me before, that I didn't know what had happened. Maybe somebody had spiked the hookah, trying to put blame on somebody else.

George simply said something along the lines of "oh. You fainted? I didn't notice. I thought you just did a really cool dance move." Aww. How cute of him. I wanted to take him home and keep him right then and there.

But, like a good story and fairy tale, that didn't happen until much much later, with plenty of twists and turns along the way.

You may be wondering where the he said/she said comes in. When I finally got up and could laugh about the situation, I rubbed my arm and realized that I was already starting to develop a very large, very painful bruise on my elbow and on my head.

Stop the music! Wait a second…. This means, that I hit the table and maybe even the floor. Which means, of course, that GEORGE DIDN'T CATCH ME WHEN I FAINTED!

All thoughts of how cute George was immediately faded from my head as I started to give him hell for not catching me. He's supposed to be a gentleman. I can't believe he didn't catch me and allowed me to fall and completely slam my head and elbow against whatever was there.

So there you have it. I have the bruises to prove that a certain *somebody* was not my knight in shining armor that night and allowed a damsel in distress to fall into the hands of the bruise dragon. And that's why I made George wait several years before I would let him trick me into thinking he was cute again. ①

關於昏倒事件，
他是這麼說的⋯⋯

by George

⋯⋯喔，我是真的有扶到她。

二〇〇四年那晚，某夜店撥放著十年前的「經典」RMB、嘻哈、流行歌曲（現在的音樂根本沒得比，老頑固筆者如是說），說實在的，我記憶很模糊了，但顯然 Janet 對當晚還歷歷在目。

我比 Janet 常跑趴，這點毋庸置疑，二〇〇四年時更是如此。酒吧夜店經驗較多的我，應該不難發現她快昏厥過去才對。儘管我們還不熟，那晚她確實異常興奮慌亂，心跳大概比音樂節奏（是經典音樂喔，別忘了）還要快上一百倍。那種表情我見多了——代表這人快癱了。

我想，我之所以沒想到 Janet 會在舞池上跌個狗吃屎，是因為她並沒喝多少酒（手裡是有一罐別人給她的啤酒，但看得出來她沒什麼喝。以前去英國的酒吧夜店，看慣大家晚上跑趴時起碼都已五杯下肚。以

Janet 的程度來看，肯定頂多只喝了手上那罐）

好吧，結果是我完全錯估了 Janet 的能耐，特別是她竟把水煙全吸進肺裡（一來是她沒經驗，二來就是我之前說的，當時她興奮異常）。這一秒，明明一臉不知所措站在舞池中，下一秒，就不支倒地了。

就在此刻，我伸手扶了她。

我得說，不曾有女生在我腳邊倒下：看到有人在面前昏倒，吃驚到失手不是沒有可能。但我絕對沒有：我千真萬確有扶她。我在想，Janet 說的瘀青，應該是扶她的反彈力所造成的：我相信，她手肘跟頭應有稍微撞到。但相信我，要是我沒扶她，撞擊力道一定更大。而我確實。有扶。

至於 Janet 說她是在我懷裡醒來，說我很可愛這點，我再同意不過。起碼這讓我知

道，跌倒沒害她眼力變差。 Ⓖ

George Young

Our first night out - he said

by George

...oh I caught her alright.

That night in 2004, in some random club that was no doubt playing what would now be called "classic" rnb, hip hop and pop tunes of the last decade (music nowadays just doesn't compare, said the old grumpy writer) was a hazy memory for me, although evidently not as hazy as it must've been for Janet.

I'm certainly a bigger partier than Janet, especially back in 2004. I frequented far more clubs and bars than she ever did, and should've known she was close to passing out, as - although I didn't know her all that well at that point in our lives - she was unusually hyper and wide-eyed, as if her heart was thumping a hundred bpm faster than the (now classic, remember) music. I'd seen that look and vibe before on people - people who were about to crash.

I think what made me consider that perhaps Janet wasn't on the verge of using the dancefloor as a face towel was that Janet hadn't drunk any alcohol (maybe she had a beer in her hand that someone bought her, but I could tell she wasn't much of a drinker - I was used to pubs and clubs in England, where people would be on their fifth drink at least by the time they were at the clubbing portion of the evening. The drink in Janet's hand was certainly her first and last of that evening.)

Well - it turned out I was utterly wrong in my assessment of Janet's stability of course, especially after she shoved the entire hookah's contents into her lungs (an action she did through inexperience and the aforementioned hyperactivity she was experiencing). One moment, Janet's standing uncertain on the dancefloor; the next, she's falling to the ground.

And that's when I catch her.

I must say, I've never had a woman literally fall at my feet before: I could've easily missed her solely due to the shock of having someone pass out in front of me. BUT I DIDN'T: I CAUGHT HER.

I think the bruising that Janet mentioned came from the snap-back caused from the catch: I

believe her elbow and head suffered a slight bump. But believe me, it would've been a much larger bump if I hadn't caught her. Which I did. Catch her, I mean.

I also agree with Janet in regards to her waking up in my arms and saying that I was cute. At least I knew her sight wasn't impaired from the fall. Ⓖ

George Young

在奧斯汀（Austin）的傳統是 1 月 1 日要去跳水，我們於是找一個住在奧斯汀的朋友 Armando 一起去。

這個泉水是冷泉，溫度永遠是攝氏 27 度左右。夏天的時候很涼爽，跳進去很涼，但因為那天的氣溫是攝氏 1 度，跳進去反而溫溫的。雖然它看起來有一點冒煙，但因為那天實在太冷了，跳下去還是感覺很冷。這行程也讓我們有機會預備一下接下來要去南極跳水的心情。

Jan.
2

這間當地做牛仔帽的店很有名，已經傳了好幾代。他們幫很多名人、藝人做過牛仔帽，比如馬龍白蘭度、克林伊斯威特……等等，很多電影裡的牛仔帽都是他們做的，而且不便宜。也有很多總統、宗教領袖訂做，比如布希總統、達賴喇嘛。那個師傅只要用手掌摸摸你的頭型、大小，就可以做得出來！

我們做完帽子後就跟他們一起去吃 BBQ。德州除了牛排很有名還有烤肋排，這間餐廳烤的肉很好吃，他們用的窯已經六十幾年，是鎮上老饕必去之處。

德州有一個主題射擊場，它仿照西部電影
場景，打造出牛仔酒吧、醫院、監獄⋯⋯
等等不同建築物，每棟建築都有可以射擊
的地方，在裡面可以玩 Cosplay、穿幾十
年前的服飾，現場所有人都很入戲。我很
喜歡我穿的這套衣服，它讓我宛如走進電
影情節裡！

這裡的槍是真的有子彈的，所以要非常小
心。我跟 George PK，當天我們比賽速度
跟準度，我很準，George 也很準，但他的
速度比我快。我們比了手槍、長槍、來福
槍射擊，分數不相上下，但因為他比我快
又輕敵，最後一不小心沒有射中，終場由
我險勝！

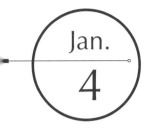

Jan.
4

奧斯汀一間老 Pub 裡有個特別的活動，叫做「雞屎賓果」，參與賓果遊戲的人可用兩塊美金買一個號碼，這些錢最後都會給贏家。店主人的媽媽養了兩隻雞，它們設計了一個大籠子，裡面有很多寫上數字的格子，接著他們放進一隻雞，看雞在哪個數字上大便，抽到那個數字的人就可以得到所有的獎金。

很好笑的是當雞開始移動，尤其走到你的號碼上面時，你會在旁邊激動地喊：「停停停，就是這邊，不要再動了！」但是等牠走掉你又會很失望，我從來沒這麼期待一隻動物大便、也從沒有一直盯著動物的屁股過！最後我們同行的朋友中了賓果，這機率很小很不可思議，不是我們為了拍攝預先設定好的喔！

我們上台領獎時，頒獎人開玩笑說：「今天你們的獎金是 125 美金，你們要這筆獎金還是我錢包裡所有的錢？」，我跟主人的媽媽說：「那當然是拿獎金啊，他的錢包怎麼可能有這麼多錢？」，他媽媽就說：「喔不不不，我兒子有時口袋裡有 500 美金喔！」

Chapter. 04

並肩
Side by Side

關係與工作的拉鋸

George 與我大概從相識到現在有百分之九十的時間都是遠距關係，所以這次五十幾天的旅程，一半工作、一半旅行，其實非常勞累，但即便如此也是我們一起待過最長的時間，所以我們很珍惜！

也因為這趟旅行，我們得以在工作的空檔，好好聊聊我們的關係與彼此的事業。我們倆都熱愛自己的工作，也很支持對方繼續在事業裡努力，所以他從不要求我放下手邊的工作去陪伴他，反之亦然。但實際上我們若要相見，勢必一方得暫時放下手邊的工作，才有辦法飛過去找對方。

我的行程通常全年度都排得滿滿的，他則是，拍戲期間時間是滿載的，沒拍戲的時候有比較大一段的空檔，在這段空檔裡，他會安排試鏡。所以，雖然看似他是比較有時間彈性的一方，但是一旦他來找我，

就是放棄試鏡的機會，以致於沒有拍戲的工作。反過來說，如果我要去找他，一定得暫時放掉工作，請假與他相聚。所以說我們經常有這些拉扯。未來我希望能夠做一些比較大的製作計劃，一次集中拍攝，留出更多的空檔來，而不是全年度持續不斷地拍攝。

有些關係裡，會有一方比較強勢，或者有一方更有決斷力，代替對方下決定，牽動著關係；這樣並沒有不好，甚至我們兩個之間或許就是欠缺這個角色、這種時刻，所以抉擇總是很艱難，即便我們都不是優柔寡斷的人。我們都非常獨立，兩個人對工作的投入程度都很高。而也因為了解彼此這點，因此也很願意支持對方的事業，以致我們對於相聚的事情，至今沒有任何的結論。我還有很多地方想去呢！George 也還有很多的可能性呢！幸好，我們兩個都是很樂觀的人，也有很多事情可以投入心力，因此這些艱難的抉擇並沒有消磨我

們的意志力，甚至成為我們好好討論彼此事業的契機。

旅途中，兩人關係新發現

Ⓙ 這次的旅行，我們有很重要的發現，那就他並不想要當外景主持人。原本我們有討論過，也許他可以一起來工作。這是南極之旅的重大發現。

Ⓖ 我不介意，只是時間長度的問題……嗯除此之外這也不是我渴望做的事情就是了。我可以偶爾做一次，但是長期、密集的旅行……還是不了哈哈。而且我還是比較熱愛演戲。

Ⓙ 這幾年都是 George 來陪我比較多，他上節目也是上我的節目。我現在有在打算放掉工作去找他，他最近接了一個美國的影集。但我是個受不了沒有工作可以做的人，所以即便是去找他，也會想辦法上他的戲哈哈！我們會試著將關係與事業重疊，因為如果不這麼做，其中一個人就得妥協。

ⓖ 這次旅行讓我們對自己有新發現，知道自己喜歡什麼、不喜歡什麼，擅長什麼、又不擅長什麼。我們發現了自己，而我發現到處去冒險不見得是我喜歡做的事情。

ⓙ 除此之外我們也發現了兩個人都不知道該怎麼辦的事，也就是剛剛談到的那些──他還是很想演戲，我還是很想去埃及、北極、這個極那個極等等的地方，而我們繼續追求這樣的生活，就還是分隔兩地。現階段而言，這根本是沒有解決的辦法。

ⓖ 我們各自的事業帶著我們去地球上不同的地方，認識這麼久，都非常習慣了。但是我們兩個都知道如果要組成家庭，勢必得做出一些改變。這次的旅程雖然很累，卻讓我們有更多時間在一起。總之以後我們就邊走邊打算吧，反正大家一有機會就會去找對方，任何機會都不放過！

溝通差異，就是要去感受對方

我們這十年來累積的友情，讓我們能夠深知對方說任何話、做任何事的脈絡；許多戀人與夫妻需要花時間磨合的事情，我們偷跑了十年！所以，我從來沒想過我們會有不和的時候。

我們兩個人的價值觀是謀合的，就算在個性與行動上會有很大的差異──我好動、他文靜，我喜歡到處移動，他喜歡待在同個地方……，我們還是能確知對方的心意。所以任何起伏，對我們而言其實就是兩個人當下狀態不同──誰能量比較弱一點，另一方就溫柔一點、體貼一點，而兩個人的狀態都很好的時候，就可以討論一些比較嚴肅或者艱難的事。雖然是截然不同的互補性格，雖然兩個人好像在溝通上有下什麼功夫，其實就只是願意用心感受對方的狀態，再站在他當時的角度思考事情而已！

離開德州後我們來到阿根廷布宜諾斯艾利斯（Buenos Aires）。阿根廷是我大學三年級留學的地方，我非常喜歡阿根廷。也因為在這邊念一年書，才對南極開始有感覺！因為要去南極會經過阿根廷，所以在阿根廷常常聽到人提起它。還記得我那時有個想法是：「什麼？南極？可以去喔？」也許就是那時被埋下第一顆種子。

我們去 Buenos Aires 做了很多在大城市會做的事，第一個是跳 Tango，那位教 Tango 的老師很辣，跳舞的時候好性感，扭動起來整個人完全投入。我原本就有學一點點 Tango，但它真的不容易，尤其是要跳得有感覺。

Buenos Aires 最有名的一區是 La Boca「彩虹屋」。就像台灣有很多日式建築,這邊許多人來自於義大利,所以彩虹屋的風格受到義大利文化影響,房子充滿繽紛的色彩。現在這一區的觀光已經發展得很好,有許多街頭藝術家聚集在這邊,很多跳Tango 的人也住在這邊。

在 Buenos Aires 我發現一個有趣的職業是幫人遛狗！那時我來台灣很想開一間這樣的公司，因為我覺得住在大城市的狗狗很可憐，沒有機會好好活動。我第一次看到這個職業時覺得怎麼這麼可愛，「遛狗人」把好幾隻小狗一起牽著走，從一個人家裡接到狗，再遛到另一個人家接其他狗，最後一起牽到公園玩，玩完之後再一路送回去各家。我在休士頓也沒看過這種職業，也許只有 Buenos Aires 有。

我覺得到 Buenos Aires 這種大城市旅行有一種玩法很有趣，就是買好幾張當地明信片之後，跟朋友一人抽幾張。接下來你們的任務就是前往你抽到明信片上面的景點，拍出一模一樣的照片！這樣很有趣也比較有目標性，就算那些景點很常見，但因為必須要找到相同角度，讓觀光變得與眾不同！

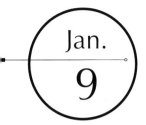

Jan.
9

在 Buenos Aires 的郊區我們去打馬球「polo」。這邊的馬每一匹都要十萬美金以上,很名貴,牠們跟德州的馬完全不同,要比功能性,你可以說德州馬是卡車,但這裡的馬就是法拉利跑車!我們去的這個牧場是演員湯姆・李・瓊斯 Tommy Lee Jones 的牧場,每一匹馬看起來雖然溫和,但一到馬場你可以感覺牠們立刻準備好!就像跑車在都市時慢慢開,但一到空曠處就可以飆車了!馬生性敏感,一般來說都不喜歡跟其他馬碰到,比如拿桿子打球時,球桿一揮出去馬通常都會怕,但是這裡的馬不一樣,當牠看到其他馬要過來搶球時,反而還會主動去撞、去防衛。

那天剛好有一群哈佛馬球隊要去打球,我跟 George 跟他們 PK,一開始我蠻擔心的,因為這邊的馬不像德州那邊會跑跑跑,轉,跑跑跑,轉,這邊的馬是一直往前衝,不會停!而且你在瞄準球時,馬還在持續移動,真的很難,需要更多的訓練。George 覺得騎這種馬反而舒服,因為牠是專業的,你會相信牠。回想不到兩個禮拜前的德州到現在,George 的騎馬技術已經進步很多了!

Jan.
10

阿根廷市區巡禮。

離開靠海的 Buenos Aires，我們搭飛機到了山上的門多薩（Mendoza）。Mendoza 位於安地斯山脈上，它海拔比較高，以美酒聞名，因此我們一起去參觀當地酒莊。這座酒莊主人叫作 Pepe，他製作的是 sparkling wine（氣泡葡萄酒）。Pepe 是一位愛笑的大哥哥，他完全投入在工作上，完全不受我們拍片的影響，而且他人超好的，後來還送我們一箱酒作為結婚禮物。

Romantic

in

Mendoza

Argentina

Jan.

13

Pepe 很喜歡 fly fishing，他帶我們去當地很美的一個湖「Laguna del Diamante」（鑽石湖），高度有近海拔四千多公尺，待久一點頭真的會暈，而湖旁的山，翻過去就是智利了，當陽光灑下來時整個湖泊亮亮的真的很像鑽石。

Pepe 的女兒會拉小提琴，她特別帶小提琴去拉給我們聽。Pepe 是一個很 sweet 的爸爸，他的女兒雖然拉得不好聽，但是 Pepe

這個大男人竟然感動得哭出來，很以他女兒為榮，女兒看爸爸哭也跟著哭了，互相擁抱說：「I love you...」，真的好感人！我們每次出去拍片都希望能與遇到的人真誠互動，而 Pepe 就是這麼真實的一個人，他不僅沒有任何商業氣息，更是百分之一百想跟我們分享所有美好的人事物。我覺得在 Mendoza 這一區的人都是這樣，很熱情！

Somewhere
Only
We
Know

我們在阿根廷又有騎馬的行程了，這邊騎馬比較像第一天在德州騎的形式，不同的是這裡並非國家公園，而是由三座山組成的私人地，放眼望去你看到的地方都是他的！

阿根廷的牛仔叫作 gaucho，相對於美國的牛仔，阿根廷的牛仔雖然不如美國牛仔那麼高壯，但是感覺更靈活一點，而且很能吃苦，他們可以住在山上一年沒問題。阿根廷牛仔吃東西很講究。光是一個 salsa 醬就要用到非常多食材，而且香腸是拿一整塊肉放進機器做絞肉，然後再塞進皮膜裡拿去烤。

紅酒對他們來說像水一樣，他們除了喝紅酒以外，也喝一種飲料叫作馬黛茶，我們在台灣一般都是用茶包泡然後倒進自己的杯子喝，但他們不是，他們是所有人共用一個杯子、一根吸管。這麼做的傳統是來自「我們是朋友、我們彼此信任」的含意。

給自己的祝福
Words to Myself

Chapter. 05

Ⓙ 你覺得,為了感情而犧牲,是什麼意思?

Ⓖ 關係裡要犧牲的是自私;其他應該沒了吧。我想有了小孩後說不定就能把自己的一切都付出,最終應該是這樣的地步,無私。

Ⓙ 真的嗎?真的沒有任何你無法為了感情拋棄的事物嗎?

Ⓖ 有,黑巧克力。不要逼我。

為愛情犧牲的多重意義

為愛情犧牲,有很多重的意思。當我年輕的時候,我曾經跟一個法國人談戀愛,那時我覺得可以為愛情放棄一切包含事業,有了事業之後才知道那根本就不是我自己,那時的我沒自信、迷失,正在經歷一場厭食症的人生風暴,不知道自己可以成為什麼樣的人。

現在我覺得,愛情裡當然會有很多習慣的改變、生活的改變,有許許多多以前做的事物不能再繼續。以前我都想衝就衝,想去哪裡就去哪裡,現在出發前需要安排與 George 見面的空檔,兩個人經常都要為對方挪動自己的計劃。但這是我欣然接受的事。我總覺得「犧牲」兩個字有一點點委屈,好像要把自己某部份殺死一樣的意思,以前我會這麼做,也許也是自願的吧,但是跟 George 在一起之後,我才領悟到改變以前的生活方式,進入兩人的關

係生活，是一種轉變，而不是犧牲。

大家都聽說過「要愛自己才懂得愛別人」的道理，我覺得那才是真正的愛喔。愛自己才知道怎麼愛別人，就像森林裡不同物種之間的共生關係，每一個物種堅強地存活下去，才有條件讓其他物種生存，反之亦然。

出自自願的妥協

過去我覺得自己無法為任何事放棄事業、放棄旅行，但我現在覺得……其實沒有什麼是無法放棄的，只是意願問題而已。

比如說自由，我願意為他放棄某部份的自由，或者說我一個人的自由。我們在一起後，我發現所謂的自由並不是一件絕對要怎麼樣的事情，而是有選擇、協商的空間。我們不會放棄的就是與對方在一起這

件事，所以這個原則就決定了我們的各種安排、選擇！一旦很清楚什麼是最重要的，那就是與對方在一起，很多事都可以再討論、調整，才能一起往同樣的地方前進。這並非不自由，因為我們的心情是願意的、快樂的。

以後有了小孩之後到底會怎樣我還不知道，不過我猜會有更多的取捨跟改變。以前我覺得自己不可能生小孩啦！我不希望生活有太大的改變啊。但是結婚之後，很多以前嘴硬的事都發現其實可以轉彎，所以我覺得，有小孩之後，這些要安排啊、協商啊、妥協的事情，應該都甘之如飴吧。有朋友曾說，有了孩子之後才知道自己有能力那樣無條件地愛一個人，這是以前從來無法想像的愛，好像生完小孩後突然長出來的一樣。我還無法體會，但是好像有那麼一點點懂了。

當然一旦在一起，做的事都要是自己喜歡的，不要下一些會讓自己討厭自己的決定。

我覺得為了他我可以變成很多樣子，為了他、為了家庭我可以放棄任何事，但是一絕對要是我自己的決定；我可以放棄自由陪他、陪家庭，別人可以批判我變得傳統了，但是如果我心甘情願，這有何不可？相對來說，如果我繼續工作，但是心裡一直焦急地想與家人在一起，這樣也不好。

總之如果我們下了一個決定，但是我們心裡無法欣然接受，表示這個決定是不可行，我們要找另一種方式。我們都能尊重彼此身為獨立的個人，這就是我們很重要的原則，也許這就是我們經常能為對方退讓而不覺得委屈的原因！

更深的牽掛與祝福

如果真的有什麼是絕對無法放棄的，那應該是性命。

以前我號稱謝大膽，去哪裡體驗或探險我都是第一個衝出去的！有的時候根本就受傷骨折了還是不肯安份，像那個時候我們去黃金海岸跑馬拉松的那趟旅程，我一開始手腕就挫傷了，一開始以為只是單純皮肉傷而已，還繼續坐越野車、潛水什麼的，後來才知道是骨折，被媽媽念很久。但是我們兩個在一起之後，我突然會想東想西，也比較會收斂一些，更注意自身安

全。同時我也無止盡地擔心著 George；我們經常飛行全世界，每次上飛機之前，都會打電話給對方講講話，而對話最後我們都會說：「千萬不要死掉。」

當你真正有個心愛的人的時候，才知道在愛中人會做出以前意想不到的事。一些浪漫的事情，那些對我來說已經是做起來不太費力的一般事情，在這些浪漫的事情之外，你永遠為對方擔心，這就是牽掛。每次只要想到他萬一發生意外，我心都很痛，而我也會想到，我如果出什麼事，他的心也會很痛。這份牽掛，我想就是付出的愛情。

就是這種擔心啦！我覺得自己都變了，出外景都會多想一下。他也是，雖然沒說出口，但是每次跟朋友出去玩，他都不會讓自己喝到醉，因為怕我擔心。這也是愛情越走越久之後的轉變，表達的方式不一樣了，牽掛的程度越來越深了。好好保有自己的性命，是我們給彼此最好的祝福。

從 Mendoza 回 Buenos Aires 拿行李，準備出發到南極。我們的路線是從 Buenos Aires 搭飛機到阿根廷最南端烏斯懷亞（Ushuaia）一這個全世界最南端的城市，聚集了全世界各地的人就像小瑞士。一月份在南半球雖然是夏天，但因為 Ushuaia 位處極南所以非常寒冷，前幾天在 Buenos Aires 還穿短袖很熱，但是現在瞬間變冬天，而且這兩種極端氣候竟然出現在同一個國家。其實 Ushuaia 位於火地島省（Tierra del Fuego），跟阿根廷是分開的。但就像蘭嶼之於台灣，雖然是同一個國家，但是去到當地又會覺得截然不同。

我們住的飯店後面有條山路宛如仙境,每一根你看到的樹木跟小樹枝都已經活了幾百年,甚至還有幾百萬年的土地,表面看起來是硬的其實是軟的。

這裡原本有一個水獺居住的區域,曾經有

商人想賣水獺的皮,從加拿大將水獺移到當地,但後來水獺繁殖太快,商人把當地數百年的樹砍掉太多,且水池淹水連帶傷害周邊居民,所以現在已經搬走。

難以突破的障礙：
George 對語言障礙的沮喪

by George

每到台灣，跟 Janet 見面、和她或我們的共同朋友出去，探索各地、嘗試新鮮事物……雖然都是件很開心的事，但總有一股疏離感如烏雲罩頂，讓人焦慮不安。

這種疏離感全來自一個因素：我中文糟透了。

我藉口很多（我相信起碼有些確實是正當理由）：我待過的國家，都不是以中文為母語（我長期待在英、美、新加坡，雖然很多新加坡人都會說中文，但英文幾乎是通用語言，所以就算只懂一點點中文也過得去）。我的作品全都講英文，有百分之九十九都必須說流利英語（普遍要講純正英國腔），只有極少例外。

時間夠的話，我幾乎都會來台跟 Janet 見面。平均每月會有幾天。因此，我也只能靠這每月短短幾天的時間，學個一兩句中文。理論上來說，要趁這三到五天練練中文當然也行，但老實說，見面時間有限，維繫感情都來不及了，實在不想耗在蝸牛爬行般學中文上面。

所以說，和 Janet 踏上五十天的拍攝旅程前，我本來擔心跟台灣攝影團隊同行，難免會有溝通障礙。果不其然。

原也以為，之後到德州、阿根廷、南極這些地方，既然母語都不是中文，靠英文應該就能暢行無阻。結果，大多時候我都錯了。

現在就一個一個來看。先說德州，我忘了考慮一項變數：我們無論走到哪，碰到的大抵是台灣人。撇開 Janet 台裔美籍的家人不說，我們的製片助理兼地陪 Jen 也是台裔美籍，跟大家都用中文溝通。而該節目的聯繫窗口之一，就是駐休士頓台北經濟文化辦事處。

上述這些人都會講英文，話雖如此，同行旅伴如果中文說得都比英文溜，又何苦大費周章跟你講英文？

即便在拍攝現場，很多時候我都是鴨子聽雷。導演 Tim 和大家都用中文溝通，我是唯一無法完全聽懂指示的人，大家一定會想說讓 Janet 翻譯給我聽。但對 Janet 來說，勢必是額外負擔，而為完成工作任務，也會造成我過度依賴她。

這也是為什麼，這個節目在錄影時，都會特別為我請一名翻譯。節目全是以英文進行，主持人要講英文，其中有一整集就在美國拍攝。

「那阿根廷呢？」你或許會問我。「你們攝影團隊的人，到那難道不會有種被疏離……或至少感到一股疏離感嗎？」

阿根廷人說西班牙語，Janet 也會這種語言。因此，西語地陪或阿根廷人有事要宣布的話，Janet 要負責幫我們翻譯，對她也是額外負擔。拜我所賜，Janet 不僅要把每一句話翻成中文或台語，還要專為在下我翻成英文。

出發到南極前，要先在烏斯懷亞拍攝，而我們找的地陪，沒錯，就是台灣人。

旅途漫漫，搭小廂型車、飛機、船、橡皮艇或騎馬往來各地，早上或晚間在飯店或住處，或者吃飯、錄影中場休息，大家總會交談聊天。看到大夥兒談天說笑、分享心得，只有我無法立即進入狀況（等我搞清楚什麼回事時，往往笑點已經過了），難免偶而會感到孤單。

要不是有通多國語言的 Janet 在，我一定會不知所措。許多方面來說，她就像我賴以遊走各國的 GPS，尤其在這充斥陌生語言的花花世界，少了我熟悉的英文，沒有

她我萬萬不能。

因此，我想要感謝：
── 首先當然是 Janet，
──Google 翻譯，
── 可離線使用的英漢字典。

同時，我深感慚愧的想表達歉意：
── 我來不及在行前把中文學好。ⓒ

The Hurdle: George's frustration with language barriers

| by George |

Whenever I'm in Taiwan, the joy of seeing Janet, hanging out with her and our friends, exploring the places and the various things one can do there...all of that is marred by an overhanging anxiety that I have of alienation.

This alienation stems from one factor: my Mandarin is poor at best.

I have plenty of excuses (and I believe that at least some of them are valid excuses): I don't live in a country where Mandarin is the go-to language (I'm in the UK, the US and Singapore most of the time, and whilst a significant number of people can and do speak Mandarin in Singapore, it's a place where practically everyone speaks English, and thus you can get by just fine not knowing a lick of Mandarin). Save for rare exceptions, the entirety of my work is in English, and 99% of that work is based on and dependant on speaking very good English (typically in a nice British accent).

I visit Taiwan to see Janet pretty much whenever I have a nice chunk of time off to do so. That is usually a few days every month. That's just enough time each month to brush up on a sentence or two of Mandarin,

and yes: I could in theory use those three to five days over there to converse largely in Mandarin, but frankly I just don't want to use up the limited time that I have with her to use it up on speaking painfully slow Mandarin, when we need this time together to maintain our relationship.

So before we embarked on this fifty day filming excursion with Janet and the Taiwanese film crew, I thought there might be a chance that there would be times where I wouldn't be able to effectively converse with everyone. I was right.

I also thought that being in Texas, then Argentina, and then Antarctica - places where you wouldn't expect the language to be predominantly Mandarin - I would be just fine and we'd all have to get along in English to get by. I was wrong most of the time on that front.

Let's look at each place in turn shall we. In Texas, it turned out that I didn't factor in the large Taiwanese contingent that we'd be meeting up with practically everywhere we went. Aside from Janet's Taiwanese American family, our assistant producer/fixer Jen was

Taiwanese American and could speak to everyone in Mandarin. One of the liaisons of the show was the Taiwanese office responsible for promoting Houston to Taiwan.

Yes - all of the above people that I mentioned could also speak English - but when the majority of your travel companions can speak better Mandarin than English, why would they speak English to us?

Even "on-set" and working, it was hard to understand what was going on a lot of the time. The director Tim would need to communicate with everyone in Mandarin, and - with me being the only person who wouldn't fully understand the instructions - most people would depend on Janet to translate everything to me. This put additional strain on Janet, and made me very dependant on her in order to do my job out there.

And that is why on this show that we were all filming - as an English speaker on an English language show, where we filmed an entire episode in the United States - I still required the services of a translator.

"But what about Argentina?" the imaginary audience in my head asks. "Wouldn't your entire team be - or at least feel - alienated there?"

Janet speaks Spanish, and they all speak Spanish in Argentina. It was therefore an additional burden on Janet to translate what the Spanish-speaking fixer and the Argentines would say to us all. And - thanks to me - not only would Janet have to translate everything once into Mandarin or Taiwanese, she'd also have to translate it into English just for Georgie Boy here.

For the filming in Ushuaia that took place just before we embarked on our journey to Antarctica, the fixer there was, of course, Taiwanese.

It was a lonely feeling at times: being left out of the conversations during the long journeys in the mini-van or plane or boat or on horseback or raft between locations, hanging out at meal times and in the hotels and apartments at the end or start of each day, or just in the moments between takes, when a joke or an observation could be shared quickly with everyone but me (and by the time it got to me the moment would have passed).

If it wasn't for Janet and her multilingual abilities, I would have been totally lost. She was and is my GPS in the world for most things, and especially in this case that involves the cluttered, overgrown jungle of another language that isn't the English to which I'm so very accustomed.

I would therefore like to thank:
- Janet obviously,
- Google Translate,
- my offline English-Chinese dictionary.

I would like to shame:
- my brain for not picking up enough Mandarin in time for this trip. Ⓖ

George Young

Ushuaia 很出名的食物是羊肉跟非常非常大的帝王蟹。我們跟一個當地居民 Jorge 一起去抓帝王蟹,那天浪很大,很多人都暈船吐到不行,當天不只船身搖晃很大,上面的攝影器材也是,我們差點被 camera crane 打到。

在那邊吃帝王蟹是現捉現煮,預先煮一鍋水,水滾了就把牠丟下去,起鍋後整隻都是你的,吃得超爽!本來負責處理帝王蟹的人要把牠內臟清掉,但我們趕快阻止他,跟他說那才是最好吃的地方,對方說一般外國人都會怕內臟,但我們就跟他說下次碰到亞洲人千萬不要清!哈哈!

我們在當地坐的是世界最南端的火車，名字叫做「The End of the World Train」，整條火車的鐵軌都是當地犯人蓋的，由於 Ushuaia 地處偏遠，所以阿根廷政府在這蓋了座監獄，以前小火車的功能是載運木頭，而那些木頭也是由犯人砍下來的；而這條鐵路就將要帶領我們前往世界最南端之地。

我們從 Ushuaia 出發南極前一天是我的生日，這也是第一次 George 爸媽跟我爸媽正式見面，他們之前只在 Skype 上簡單見過面。那天也是所有去南極參加婚禮的人第一次見面，我的朋友從世界各地聚集在這裡，但是 George 只有爸爸媽媽去參加，他的朋友不是說沒空就是太貴或無法請假，所以 50 個人扣掉工作人員，剩下 41 個人全都是我朋友。為了彌補 George 的遺憾，當天我準備給 George 一個大驚喜，送給他當作結婚禮物。

幾個月前我偷偷飛去倫敦找他的好朋友，幫 George 拍了一段影片，讓他有一個難忘的虛擬「單身趴」！在那個影片裡我打扮成一個脫衣舞孃，假裝在一個房間裡跟男士們調情，一邊脫衣服一邊拿鞭子出來，接著隔天男士們在床上醒來，有人還銬著手銬、另外一個滿臉都是吻痕，再另一個手上拿著保險套……大家一頭霧水前晚到底發生什麼事？接著鏡頭有雙穿著網襪的腿出現，畫面慢慢帶到臉上時，我出現了。這時原本看著影片非常感動的 George 瞬間愣住，張口結舌地說：「妳……妳怎麼會在這裡？……妳什麼時候去倫敦？這是真的嗎？」給他很大的驚喜，他真的很開心。但是最大的驚喜還在後面。我說服他最好的朋友來到現場！當 George 最好的朋友 William 打開門出現的那一剎那，George 完全震驚了！

擇偶條件
Checking the Boxes

by George

Janet 讓我成為更好的人。

小至穿什麼,大至重要的人生規劃,碰到做決定,我都很容易猶豫不決。是 Janet 讓我知道,不是什麼決定都攸關生死:寧可做決定,踏前一步,也不要優柔寡斷,滯步不前。

Janet 非常好相處,和誰都能打交道,加上很有親切感,人緣極佳。怪不得,天生是走演藝圈的料。至於我……偶而也這樣,但只限心情好的時候。尤其之前錄影,跟大家朝夕相處五十多天下來,發現她對每件事都充滿熱情,像潤滑劑一樣,能讓大家打成一片,說真的,要不是我親眼目睹,還真不敢相信。我甚至常希望,跟她在一起久了,說不定能感染一點她的性格。

其實剛剛交往沒多久,我就在想,我想跟這個人共度一輩子。我一直尋尋覓覓這樣的人:有自信、有幽默感、平易近人……而最重要的,聽到我的笑話會笑。這些條件她都具備。

我以前常說,情侶和夫妻唯一的差別,在於後者戴的首飾稍微多一點,但老實說,我現在發現,差別可大呢。

婚前的我,歷經過兩階段的自信:二十歲的我,魯莽、輕率、膽大包天、狂妄自大(告別青少年時期的不安全感);三十歲的我,較瞭解自己是怎樣的人,因此擁有一種較內斂世故的自信。

如今,婚後的我,則變成一種更成熟、穩重的自信。生活突然間有了安定感;「尋找真命天子/天女」的選項既然打勾了,就可以去追尋其他人生目標了,而且,不再是一個人。ⓒ

Janet makes me a better person.

I've always been terrible at making decisions: from what to wear, to major career decisions. But Janet's been helping me realise that not every decision is life and death: it's better to move forward by making a decision, than to be paralysed by indecision.

Janet's also extremely easy to get along with - she can socialise with anybody, and has this approachable personality that people enjoy. That's why she's such a good TV personality. I am like that…occasionally, and only if I'm in the right mood for it. Especially during the fifty or so days of filming together, I've seen this enthusiasm for all things and all people permeate through Janet to a degree that I would think incredible if I hadn't witnessed it with my own two eyes. I'm consistently hoping that that part of her personality rubs off on me the more I hang out with her.

When we were dating, it was pretty early on that I thought I could be with this person for the rest of my life. I always looked for confidence, a sense of humour, personability…and most importantly: someone who laughed at my jokes. She checked all those boxes.

I've often said that the only difference between being an unmarried couple and being married is that the latter requires you to wear a little more jewelry, but really - I've found that there is a more substantial change.

In my life prior to marriage, I've experienced two stages of confidence: the raw, brash, fearless and unchanneled confidence of your 20s (replacing the insecurities of one's teenage years), and the more refined and focused confidence that's found in your 30s, when you've discovered more about who you are as a person.

Now - post-marriage - I'm experiencing a more mature confidence and stability in my life. You're instantly more settled; the box that's labelled "find Mr/Mrs Right" is checked, and you can get on with everything else on life's To Do list, together. Ⓖ

我們在南極要搭的俄羅斯籍破冰船，世界只有兩艘這樣規模的船，它除了破冰功能外還有一個訊號發射器，是冷戰時期非常有價值的間諜船！

這次去阿根廷和大學時的感覺差很多，那時一 peso 等於一美金，整個國家的素質很高、東西也貴，在美洲算是有錢的國家。但我畢業那一年 2000 年經濟政治崩壞，對美元的幣值從 1 比 1 變成 1 比 10，整個國家大亂、銀行擠兌，接著十幾年整個國家狀態都不太好。雖然現在 1 比 6 有好一點，但跟我大學時比起來還是差太多了。記得大學在阿根廷買東西時，當地人不見得要美金，因為 peso 有時還比較強勢，那時經濟很好、不會有很多遊民、治安像台灣一樣很安全、街上也不會有很多店關閉，但這次去就有很大的差異，你會開始發現有些地區比較危險、整個城市變得比較髒、越來越多遊民睡在路上、建築物缺乏整修、破破爛爛的……

回顧從德州一路往南，我們經歷了北半球的冬天、接著到阿根廷熱得要命的夏日氣候、又到海拔四千多公尺極凍的高山，再來一路往南到 Ushuaia 接近南極的寒冷氣候，那種感覺真的很妙，經歷了完整的四季。而且整趟旅程有野外玩水、騎馬行程，也有城市需要高跟鞋的行程，所以出發前整理衣服需要很高超的技巧！

如何維繫關係：
請多多善用激將法
（不是對小孩才管用喔！）

by George

大家的爸媽應該都說過下面（或至少類似）的話：

「好吧，花椰菜你就別吃了。它對你身體太好，我可不希望你長得太高太壯。」

這番話，就像在對你下神奇咒語般：會控制你的身心，驅使你去執行一項任務——幾秒之前，打死你也不肯去做——然後，耶：滿嘴都是花椰菜。

好吧，這些年來，就我對 Janet 的認識（超過十年，持續累積中），神奇激將法對她也管用。而這件事，我主要是透過吵架發現的。

吵架並非導火線。從來不是這樣，對吧？（沒錯！錯！瞧，我們開始吵了！）

語氣才是導火線：每當我運用話術，帶點爭論的語調說話（再微乎其微都會被 Janet

抓到，相信我），她就會開始自我防衛，刻意跟我唱反調。

舉例來說，我跟 Janet 有時會爭個面紅耳赤，就是因為個性上有一個鮮明差異：她是那種冒險犯難的熱血性格，我則恰恰相反——有些人可能會覺得，我對每件事都常過度謹慎。

我說 Janet 啊，大本德國家公園的岩石路又高又陡，妳在那邊騎馬，應該戴堅固的安全帽，而不是那種軟趴趴、毫無防護力的牛仔帽。啊哈：結果 Janet 偏偏戴牛仔帽騎馬。

Janet，德雷克海峽可是有名的「世界洗衣機」，在那裡乘風破浪可不是好玩的，妳應該吃點暈船藥。呃：結果 Janet 什麼藥都沒吃。

Janet，我能不能建議，我們還是別坐平底

雪橇滑下山壁吧，那裡山壁簡直陡得跟劍插在地上一樣，當地可是連一間公立醫院都沒有喔！結果，啾碰：在南極大陸一路仆街滑下去。

不過，這當然是雙方的。Janet 總是不經意的說服我做些違背己意的事，而我會被說動，完全是出於賭氣。嗯，起碼我是希望那是不經意的。

身為聰明人，就要懂得用激將法來操縱一個人的行為。我相信，作為夫妻的我們適用，將來萬一有後代，這招也會行得通；父母那輩是這麼過來的，祖父母當然也不例外。

所以，人要識相，千萬別推薦你朋友看這一本書，否則你朋友只會覺得你太夠意思了，沒人會想做人太夠意思吧？ⓖ

Relationship advice: the art of reverse psychology

(It's not just for kids!)

by George

Remember when your mum or dad said the following words (or at least, something very similar):

"Fine - don't eat that broccoli - it's too good for you anyway and I don't want you growing up too big and strong".

It's as if they incanted the most magical of spells on you: one that takes over your mind and body, and compels you to perform a task that - only a few seconds ago - you were certain you'd never do...and then bam: mouth full o'broccoli.

Well, I've discovered over the years that I've known Janet (over a decade and counting), that the magic of reverse psychology can work wonders on her too. And I've mainly discovered this through arguments.

They don't start off as arguments. They never do, do they ("yes they do! No they don't! And now we're arguing!")

It's the tone that's the trick: whenever I say something that's in the argumentative scale of the music that is the art of conversation (and Janet can pick up on the merest sliver of argumentative tone, believe me), she'll switch to defensive mode and do whatever the exact opposite is of what I said or suggested.

For instance - let's pick something out of the relationship that that's a common contrast between Janet's and my personality, and thus can sometimes lead to heated conversations: her adventurous and gung-ho demeanour, versus my - some would say - over-cautious attitude towards all things.

Janet: you should wear a hard helmet when horse riding along these very high rock paths around Big Bend, and not that soft and not-protective-at-all cowgirl hat. Shazam: Janet on a horse in a cowgirl hat.

Janet perhaps you should take these sea sickness pills whilst we go get battered through the washing machine of the world that's more formally known as Drake's Passage. Whizz: Janet completely medication-free.

Janet, might I suggest that we don't toboggan down an impressively-steep mountain face - yes the one that's jutting out like Inuit Ice God Nootiakok's

dagger- from a land that consists of exactly zero government hospitals? Pazzow: slip and slide on the far side of the planet.

It works both ways of course. Janet has inadvertently convinced me to do a complete u-turn on my intentions just because I'm annoyed with her. At least, I'd like to think it was inadvertent.

What the smarter folk do is purposefully use this reverse psychology to manipulate one's actions. I'm sure all this practice that we're getting in as a couple will help us utilise this trickery on our progeny should some ever sprout forth; as it was with our parents before us, and their parents before them.

Now be a dear and don't recommend that your friend read this book - it'll only make you a more valuable life companion in their eyes, and who wants to be too valuable? Ⓒ

George Young

看到 William 現身在世界盡頭，George 的反應是……

by George

普遍說來，我不是個愛驚喜的人。接受驚喜也好，製造驚喜也罷；驚喜對我而言，就是驚過於喜。

我認為，驚喜的重點在於，把一個人暫時拋出舒適圈外。而我，偏偏就討厭這種受驚的感覺，寧願享受平靜無波的安逸。

好幾次，Janet 製造驚喜，就給我和家人惹來麻煩。譬如有一次，Janet 出其不意來新加坡，想給我來個驚喜，卻犯了一個錯，那就是先跟我弟講，結果他告訴了我（我們全家都不喜歡被突然造訪，這點我弟清楚）。Janet 發現驚喜被破壞，跟我大吵一架。

諸此之類的突擊事件（是突擊沒錯）三番兩次引發爭吵，但顯然都沒讓 Janet 打退堂鼓，依然故我，甚至不惜數月籌備一場大驚喜，打算把我嚇個正著。

那是二〇一五年一月二十日的前幾個月。一月二十日是 Janet 生日，也是南極行的前一天，我們要在烏斯懷亞市舉辦婚禮派對。南極行的前幾個月，Janet 照理說是在德國工作，我渾然不知她瞞著我，飛到倫敦，串通我好幾個以前在校最要好的朋友，拍攝一支驚喜短片，算是送給我的另類單身派對，是只有主角我缺席的那種（我才懶得辦這種東西，你也知道……我去的派對夠多了）。

二〇一五年一月二十日這天到了。我跟 Janet 事前準備了一支音樂錄影帶，要讓賓客在遠征南極的船上模仿，預計要在我們為來賓致詞前播放。而就在我傻傻等待大螢幕出現這支錄影帶時，事情發生了。

結果錄影帶沒播，反倒突然冒出以前學校朋友的聲音，接著一張張我的囧照出現在螢幕上，落為在場眾人的笑柄。這下，我被 Janet 擺了一道。

囧照才放完，緊接著就是剛才說的另類單身派對短片，演出者包括我好幾位朋友、一名前女友、一張貼有本人照片的瓦楞紙人像，以及本片最大驚喜——Janet。

Janet 竟然到倫敦找我那群倫敦朋友，我簡直不敢相信。當時我臉上的表情，難以用文字來形容。

不過，所幸（抑或不幸的是）你就算人不在場，也不會錯過精彩片段。拜當代驚人科技發展所賜，人人手邊都有拍攝設備，有關上述事件的照片、影片多不勝數。

短片播畢，Janet 提醒我，我的苦難還沒結束。

要發現 William 的身影不難——身高六呎七吋（二百零一公分），腰圍也不遑多讓。應該說，藏他比不藏他還困難，所以說，他從側門走進會場時，想不看到都難。

William 是唯一我單方邀來參加南極婚禮的朋友。

後來才知道，Janet 為隱瞞 William 會出席的事，從頭到尾都讓他使用化名：所有電子郵件、書信往返，真名只有她跟領隊知道（領隊會全程參與南極長征，難怪她自信滿滿，這次她參與籌備的行程會樂趣無窮）。

Janet 以為整場下來總會戳到我的哭點：若看到獻給我的單身派對短片沒哭，起碼看到 William 現身於烏斯懷亞會哭。但，結果兩者都沒令我掉淚，反而是讓我嘖嘖稱奇，Janet 究竟是何方神聖，敢背著我策劃這一連串祕密行動。

至於那天接下來，她是不是又使出什麼招數，逼我淚水潰堤，告訴你吧，沒有：一月那天，我只有一臉傻眼。ⓒ

Reaction to William's appearance at the End of the World

by George

I don't generally like surprises. Whether it's me receiving them, or me doling them out: in my mind, surprises are unsettling.

I suppose that's the point of surprises: to jolt you out of your comfort zone for a moment in time. For me however, I dislike jolts, and rather enjoy the comfort that I mentioned in the earlier sentence.

My family and I have gotten into trouble before with Janet and surprises. Namely, one time when Janet tried to organise a surprise visit to Singapore to catch me unawares. Janet made the mistake of telling my brother, and he told me (as he knows us Ng's do not like being caught unawares). Janet discovered that the surprise was ruined and arguments ensued.

Evidently, these arguments from past surprise attacks (for they are attacks) did not dissuade Janet from subsequent attempts, as she instigated a plan that took at least a few months in the making to get me good.

A few months before the 20th January 2015 - Janet's birthday, and the date our wedding party were assembled in Ushuaia the eve before embarking on our journey to Antarctica - Janet was supposedly in Germany on a work trip. Unbeknownst to me however, Janet was actually in London town, with many of my closest school friends, filming a rather dodgy short film that was to be the stag party that I would never experience first-hand (I never bothered arranging one you see...I party enough anyway).

Back to the 20th January 2015: Janet and I are giving a speech to our guests, and I'm waiting for a music video to appear on the big screen: a music video that both Janet and I want our guests to emulate on the ship during our Antarctic expedition.

Instead of this music video, I suddenly hear the voice of one of my school friends, and once I see the third of a number of embarrassing pictures of myself pop up on screen for all to laugh at, I realise I was in for one of Janet's surprise attacks.

Following the embarrassing pictures was the aforementioned stag video, which starred several of my friends, an ex-girlfriend, a cardboard cut out of Yours Truly, and - what was to be the biggest shock of the video - Janet.

I can't use words to describe the look on my face; the sheer sense of disbelief I expressed when I saw Janet there in London, with my London friends.

Fortunately (or unfortunately), this isn't one of those "you had to be there" moments as, thanks to the wonders of recording technology that lie in our disposal, there are plenty of photographs and video of the event in question.

After the video ended, Janet warned me that my tribulations were not over.

It's not hard to catch sight of William - he's six foot seven and almost as wide. In fact, it's harder to hide him, so it was all the more impressive when he emerged through the side entrance of the venue. William was to be the one friend who was purely from my side of the invitation list to show up to my Antarctic wedding.

Turns out that, in order to hide William's attendance, he was under a pseudonym throughout. In all the emails and all the correspondence, his real identity was known only to Janet and the tour coordinator

(who also happened to be coming with us on this excursion, which come to think of it is a testament to her confidence that the trip she helped organise was going to be lots of fun).

Janet was expecting me to cry at some point: if not during the stag video that was made in my honour, then at the point when William showed up in Ushuaia. But these two events didn't move me to tears - they moved me to wonder just how in the hell Janet has the moxy to plan this whole sequence of covert events without my knowledge.

I suppose the worry about all the possible things that she could or would do to me next should've brought on the waterworks at that point, but nope: it was pure dumbfoundedness on my face that day in January. ©

Chapter. 06

兩個人一起的冒險
One Guy, One Girl, One Adventure

旅行傾向完全相反的兩個人，決定要去南極結婚？！

這幾年因為工作，我真正一個人旅行的機會並不多，主要都是跟拍攝團隊一起工作，我很喜歡團隊一起工作的感覺。這次 George 來一起工作，則是這幾年以來我們兩個在一起相處最長的時間吧！

關於旅行，我跟 George 的偏好和傾向都是相反的兩極 我對任何冒險一向來者不拒，他則是對任何有一點點危險氣息的事情，或者是聞到一點點挑戰的味道，都會在心中嘀嘀咕咕；但是這次的 51 天、史詩式、橫跨三大洲的結婚大冒險之旅，居然是出自他一句玩笑話。

當時我的爸爸媽媽正在研究去南極的郵輪旅行，他們跟朋友一起報名了旅行團，他們問我要不要去，並且把行程表寄給我。我一看到團費跟行程，馬上一通電話叫他們取消報名，我們自己來一原來旅行團的行程實在太貴，也實在很少真正著墨南極。於是當我回神過來的時候，發現……我的房間牆壁上早已貼滿了不同郵輪公司的資訊。

我問 George 要不要一起來，心中覺得應該會被否決吧哈哈。我接著又問他，既然你受到邀請了，那不如邀請你父母一起來，反正雙方父母沒見過面，乾脆藉這個機會見面。George 開玩笑地回答：「既然雙方父母都會到場，既然我們見面的機會那麼少，那乾脆在南極結婚也不錯。」

他當然、沒有料到、我當真了。當然，他事後一定心想，早該知道 Janet 會當真，而且會付諸行動；他早該知道，只要在我腦袋裡種下去南極的種子，它就會一直長大、一直長大，直到開花結果的時刻來臨！

個性互補的溝通藝術

我跟 George 就是標準的互補性格，或者根本就是相反的個性。他不喜歡意外、不喜歡危險、不喜歡驚喜，驚喜對他而言，應該是驚大過喜吧！我還記得有一次我要給他一個驚喜，但不幸地我向他弟弟透露，而他的弟弟深知哥哥不喜歡驚喜，事先通報，於是消息走漏，我們吵了一架哈哈！

我們是如此不同，他很謹慎，我偏偏經常不聽勸。剛開始談戀愛的時候，我們會有很多很多的爭吵（說是爭吵，其實也只是兩個人你一言我一語），他說什麼，最後我就會做相反的事，我提議什麼活動，他要考慮很久，在這過程中大大小小的角力，諸如此類。當然我們也很樂在其中，這是了解彼此也了解自己的過程。

在這過程當中，我們竟然都慢慢地互相搭

配得很好了！他懂得要用什麼樣的話術，讓我一步步落入他的「圈套」，就好像從小到大，爸媽用各種方式引誘我們吃下不好吃的青菜那樣的方式哈哈！而我居然也讓他踏上了長達五十一天、充滿驚奇與新發現的旅程。

兩個人各自的旅程，
也是一起的旅程

我一直覺得自己就算是一個人旅行，也不是一個人旅行。旅途出發前，我會跟朋友討論；旅途中，我時時向家人、朋友報告見聞，也總是會得到大家熱烈的回應；遇到困難的時候，異地總是有一些陌生人，對我伸出援手，我不是一個人，而他們往往也變成朋友。

旅行如此，人生也如此。雖然我一直是很獨立的人，但我常常覺得每個人都很不

同，在一起的時候，總是能夠發生不一樣的事情，因為很多事情你想得到的我不一定能想到，這個時候，就會覺得跟別人在一起很好。不一定是同一個人，有些事我會跟媽媽商量，有些事我只想跟姐姐講，而有的時候又是朋友、同事…人永遠不是自己一個人，身邊一定會有別的人，只是來來去去罷了。

現在生命裡有了 George，我大部份的事情都是跟他聊，大部份的時候都是有他陪伴。以前一個人的時候，難免會有身邊沒有任何人的時候；有了 George 之後，我心裡就不覺得自己是一個人了，就算我自己一個人的時候，也覺得自己不是一個人。這樣讓人有安全感。

兩個人的旅程與新的發現

跟個性互補（其實是截然不同、甚至是相反的個性！）的 George 在一起，我發現了許多以前不會去想的事，而他跟我在一起以後，也做了很多以前根本不能想像的事。

我曾經成功說服他跟我去東加的一趟為期十天的風帆之旅，而他說服我飛去舊金山找他，兩個人什麼特別的行程都沒有安排，就是待在一起而已。這次的旅程，我成功說服 George 在德州跟阿根廷都各騎了一次馬，而他帶我去看位於德州 Marfa 的裝置藝術…。而最令我驚奇的，就是 George 願意跟我一起，在南極露營一要知道，這件事意味著在水桶裡上廁所並且最後必須打包帶走，晚上會有一大堆海豹在你四周跟彼此聊天、挖洞睡覺、永畫……。然後還有跳到非常、非常、非常冰凍的南極之水裡。我們活下來了。我想如果 George 知道跟我結婚的下場是到南極跳冰水，他可能會再更仔細地考慮要不要結婚吧！

話雖如此，雖然人們都說我比 George 敢衝、我比 George 勇敢，他也說自己很謹慎，但是我認為謹慎絕對不等於怯懦——而這趟旅行，他也證明了這一點。我們從德州、阿根廷一直到南極圈的旅行，很令人畏懼，也深具挑戰性——跟未來一樣，無論是我們各自的未來，或是我們兩個人共同的未來。對於這次的旅途，George 說：「進入未知領域的旅程、無止盡的旅行、無止盡的拍攝期程等等，都令人疲累，但經過這次的旅行，我們終將成為更強大的一對戀人，強大到足以面對這一切。」George 在婚禮上告訴我，我讓他勇於挑戰未知，讓他有勇氣告訴一個女人他有多愛她。我則要說，他遠遠超越我過去所有身體的冒險，讓我學習到勇氣與謹慎結合時的強大力量；他讓我明白，什麼是真正的勇氣。

從阿根廷離開，緊接著是整整 11 天的南極行程，出發前我看了許多南極資料，當地規定蠻嚴格的，尤其是船，一個地方只能進去一艘、一次只能上岸一百個人。我們可以挑小船、中船或是大船，大船最舒服，不會暈船，可搭 500 至 1000 人，但我想如果一次只能上岸 100 個人，等於每人只有 30 分鐘，這樣不太合適；而小船類似帆船，每次可乘 20 至 50 人，但是開的時間太長而且會很暈，我完全不考慮。最後我選擇中船，它可以容納 100 至 150 人，雖然沒那麼豪華、無法邀請太多人，但是最合適，而且它是研究型「間諜」船，全世界只有兩艘，我覺得很酷於是便選了它。

南極旅程沒有辦法確實安排每天要做的事情，因為要看天氣，還有看船長依照天候決定在那裡停⋯⋯有太多影響的因素。我們那本寫滿旅程要聯絡誰、住哪裡、要做什麼的「Bible」（拍攝行程小寶典），在德州、阿根廷部分寫得密密麻麻，但是到南極竟然完全空白！因為我們在南極要等到前一天才能跟船長討論隔天去哪、天氣大概如何、可以做什麼⋯⋯等等。

船長很可愛，他會在報告完以上情況後問我們說：「你們明天想結婚嗎？」我們就會問：「那你覺得怎樣？」他常常回答：「明天是不錯啦⋯⋯但後面的天氣、環境可能更好⋯⋯不過⋯⋯你們確定還要等嗎？」哈哈！所以我們每天都超掙扎的，但還是會一直拖，而且越拖越緊張！所以導演那段時間超擔心的，他想怎麼可能在完全沒有 rundown 的情況下就出發去拍？而且連婚禮哪一天都不知道！？

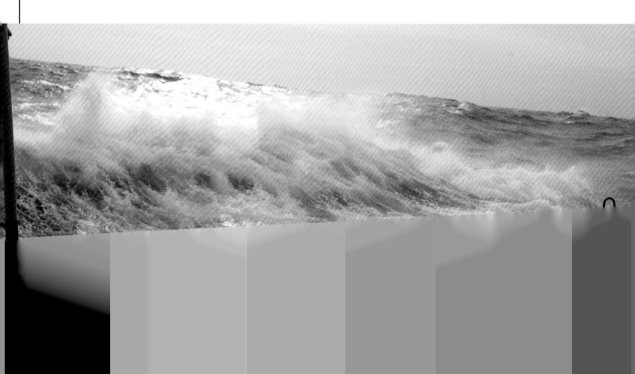

從阿根廷到南極中間海域是太平洋、大西洋、南極海的匯集交界處,浪特別大,可以說是全世界最險惡的海域,這裡還有一個特別的稱號:「世界的洗衣機」。我跟George 打賭,我們不吃暈船藥、不用暈船貼片、不戴防暈環,看誰先暈船,結果我們兩個都是不會暈船的體質!其實到那天為止已經連拍三個禮拜,很緊繃,既然海上沒什麼既定拍片行程,我們就整個放鬆下來,而且手機完全沒有訊號,如果有第三次世界大戰也不會知道!那兩天過得很舒服,你有自己的空間、往外看是一望無際的海,我們的船六層樓高,但浪比船更高,光看浪就覺得很酷!

我們在船上吃得很好,有俄羅斯廚師為我們準備三餐,早餐是自助式 buffet,午餐則是先點主餐,到餐廳再吃沙拉吧,如果因為暈船沒辦法吃,還可以外帶。船後面設有零食、咖啡自助吧,讓所有客人自由享用。

那幾天沒有手機真的差很多,我們有很多時間坐下來跟爸爸媽媽、朋友聊天,在房間也不能滑手機,無時無刻都是活在當下,好喜歡這種感覺!如果朋友沒有暈船,我們就會聚集在後面玩撲克牌、寫明信片、寫日記、拍照,很單純地生活,很棒的感覺……沒有手機,你找不到別人、別人也找不到你,這在現實生活中太難得了!

在南極結婚的所有擔心也要放掉，因為你不知道哪一天的天氣適合結婚，反而不用像一般新娘張羅那麼多瑣事，還要擔心會跟爸爸媽媽吵架，完全不用想這些。反正衣服準備好了、珠寶回來了，就完全沒有壓力了。

當船漸漸靠近陸地，搖晃得比較小，船上朋友們也一個一個出來活動。我們的船長告訴我們，一直到第七天還有人對船上遇到的人說：「咦！你也有來啊！？」哈哈！

看到陸地那一瞬間還蠻開心的，那就是傳說中的南極耶！接著開始有企鵝在那邊走動好可愛。我們笑說當你看到第一隻企鵝出現時會先拍個一百張照片，但是後面一整群出現時……你根本就拍不完！我本來就很喜歡企鵝，所以去南極前狂看好多南極跟企鵝的影片，我群組裡的朋友都快被我煩死了，動不動就傳企鵝的影片給他們！但是真正到南極才發現企鵝很吵也很臭！在動物園看到的企鵝白白的，好像穿西裝，但那邊不是。企鵝會在自己家大便，

大完便後還躺在自己的大便上取暖，所以整身都是便便，臭臭的！牠們唯一乾淨時是跳到海裡捕魚的時候，會順便把自己洗得黑白分明。

我們每天都有兩個行程，早上會先靠岸一次，讓大家上岸玩個三小時，下午再去另一個地方走走，船長則在我們吃午餐的時候移動到下一個點。在南極有一個規矩是，你不能留任何的東西在陸地上，連上廁所也不行，要保持百分之百的乾淨，你也不能拿走任何東西，連企鵝大便都不行拿，要把自己當成鬼魂一樣！

南極半島有個「欺瞞島」（Deception Island），因為它是隨時都會爆發的活火山，所以也感覺比較暖和。以前有人在這邊蓋了一座小城市，專門煉鯨魚油跟銷售，現在看到的廢墟都是之前煉油廠留下來的。因為好多鯨魚被騙進去那個峽灣殺掉，所以那個地方才叫「欺瞞島」。

在這邊為了煉油所以要生火，但沒有木柴怎麼辦？他們竟然拿企鵝當作燃料來燒！因為企鵝很肥，全身百分之八十以上都是脂肪！

我們玩了跳水「Take the Plunge」。「Take the Plunge」有一個雙關語是「豁出去／結婚」。那邊的水真的會冷、會刺痛，但從水裡出來的那瞬間是暖的，大約過了十秒接觸到空氣之後就會開始發抖。

飛蛾撲「水」（成語）：
寓意就是，跟某人結婚，交出自己

by Janet

如果真要問我，我或許得承認一件事，那就是，其實早在去南極很久很久以前，我就決定要「飛蛾撲火」了。老實說，跟 George 約會才一個月左右，我就知道自己麻煩大了。

記得 George 曾對我說（當時我們才約會不久）：「小心別愛上我了。」那時我就心想：「啐！這傢伙真不要臉，竟敢告訴我什麼該做、什麼不該做？！」但一個月後，固執又叛逆的我，決定跟 George 作對，他要我別愛上他……我就偏要愛上他。哈！活該！誰叫你敢告訴我什麼不該做。哇哈哈哈哈哈哈哈！

所以，就本案而言，我贏了。也可以說，是 George 贏了，畢竟，我愛上他了。好吧，都好。我們都贏了。

跟 George 約會大概一個月左右，我就知道自己瘋狂愛上他了，想跟他共度一輩子。沒

這類經驗的人，聽我這麼說一定覺得很矯情。然而，這種感覺一旦出現……是擋也擋不住的。我以前當然也跟別人約會過，有時也會有瘋狂愛上某人的錯覺，但總會感到哪裡不太對勁。你會想說，再嘗試一下下，再決定要不要交出自己。而跟 George 在一起時，就沒有這層障礙在。我毫無保留，義無反顧，也清楚知道，要是我們走不到最後，我的心情一定會像乘雲霄飛車，然後跌落谷底。

基本上，我甚至有隨時私奔的打算——只要時間地點對了，啪！我隨時都願意飛蛾撲火！雖然等了些時日才在南極一塊飛蛾撲火，但容我爆料，其實在婚禮前幾天，我們就先在南極「撲水」了。

記得是一月二十三或二十四日。當你也一天當兩天用，加上又沒有什麼 3C 產品可查日期、幾點幾分，就容易把日子混淆在一塊。先前有人告訴過我們，南極有地方可以泡溫

泉，是活火山的火山運動把水加熱所形成的，溫度剛好可以游泳。

我們對正宗南極跳水都躍躍欲試，之前在德州奧斯丁嘗試過元旦極地跳水，水沒有想像中溫。老實說，是冷爆了！一出水就抖到不能自己，這還只是在德州奧斯丁！是德州喔——德州啊，我的家鄉……你怎麼捨得這麼對我……。

好吧，我離題了。回到南極。我們啟程前往「欺瞞島」（譯註：此為英文原名「Deception Island」的意譯，又英譯為「迪塞普遜島」），島上有溫泉，對陸地和水有加溫效果。地熱作用下，黑色沙灘蒸氣繚繞，乍看之下，你絕對想不到這是在南極！在我們好說歹說下，一票朋友終於肯一起去跳水。我們早就想好在水裡要玩什麼，譬如騎馬打仗、假裝是噴泉雕像，然後拍照之類的。一定會終身難忘。

我們決定要一起上陣，以團隊力量相互給與精神與實際上的支持，免得到南極跳水時有人臨陣脫逃。數到一、二、三……大夥剝洋蔥般一層層脫去衣服（防風防水戰術外套、厚羽絨冬季外套、長袖發熱衣、小背心、圍巾、毛帽、保暖手套、防風防水褲、半防水滑雪褲、發熱衛生褲、保暖內層襪、厚毛襪，最後是軟膠雨靴），然後噗通跳入水中。

原本計劃好要游個幾圈、擺姿勢拍照、慢動作潑對方水，結果都不了了之，我們大家一路尖叫入水，泡沒幾下又一路尖叫逃回陸地。與其說是「游泳」，不如說是一群「跳進融冰、驚聲尖叫的瘋子」。

這種椎心刺骨的冰冷，是從來沒有過的。水冰到會燙人。簡直凍死人了。我覺得再待上四十秒，手腳恐怕都會壞死。

說好的溫泉呢？不是說有溫泉可以泡進去、好好放鬆一番嗎？我們都覺得被欺騙了！現

在，我們總算知道，這座島為何叫「欺瞞島」
了。不過，我們至少辦到了。無論如何，我
們都心一橫，跳入全世界數一數二的冰水，
而且活著回來，訴說這段故事。沒錯，我們
都「撲水」了。

早知道跟我在一起，不僅要去南極走透透，
還要去極地冰水裡游泳，George 恐怕會打退
堂鼓，猶豫要不要「再」跟我一起「飛蛾撲
水」。但，都到了這時候，反悔已太遲：他
曾警告我別愛上他，卻忘了告誡自己：千萬
別愛上我。①

Take the plunge (phrase): meaning, to marry someone, to commit oneself

by Janet

If you were to really ask me, I'd probably have admitted to have "taken the plunge" waaaaay before Antarctica even happened. It was honestly probably just a month after starting to date George that I knew I was in trouble.

I remember George telling me (as we had just started to date): "Be careful. Don't fall in love with me." and my thoughts after that were something along the lines of "Psh! Who is this guy telling me what to and not to do?!" But after a month, me with my stubborn and subordinate nature, I decided to defy George's orders to NOT fall in love with him…and I fell in love with him. Ha! There! That's what you get for trying to tell me what NOT to do. PBTHTHTHththththth!

So, in this case, I won. Or I guess George won because now I'm in love with him. Ok fine: we both won.

After about a month of dating, I knew that I was not only madly in love with George but I wanted to be with him forever and ever. I know it sounds cheesy to people who haven't experienced it before, but when you know.. you just know. I have dated previously

and sometimes you feel like you're madly in love with someone, but there's always a hint of something that's just not right. You want to test it out a little bit longer before you allow your heart to make any deeper commitments. With George, I didn't have that barrier. I didn't have those reservations. I just jumped straight into it knowing full well that if things didn't work out, my heart was going to be in for one hell of a rollercoaster ride of emotions.

Basically, I was ready to elope at any point - we just had to find the right place, time and bam! I was ready to take the plunge. It would take awhile longer before we actually took the plunge in Antarctica, but let me first tell you about another Antarctic plunge that we took just a few days before our actual wedding.

I believe it was January 23 or 24th. Our days kind of become all blurred together when you're living each day as if it were two days, and there's also very little technology to tell you the time of day or even the day of the year. We had been told of thermal hot springs in Antarctica of all places. Somewhere where the volcanic activity in the ACTIVE volcano would heat up the water to the point where you could go for a swim!

We were both excited about this since we had just previously done a New Year polar plunge in Austin, Texas, where the water wasn't as warm as we had imagined. In fact, it was freaking freezing! I was shaking uncontrollably by the time I got out of the water. And that was Austin, Texas!! TEXAS - my home state...how could you do this to me, Texas...

Anyway, I digress. Back to Antarctica. We were about to go to Deception Island, where these thermal hot springs would heat up the land and the water. The black sand beaches were steaming from these underground thermals and it just looked unlike anything you would ever imagine seeing in Antarctica! We had managed to convince a whole group of our friends to do this plunge with us. We had ideas of how we would all play in the water, play chicken fight, pretend to be statuettes in a fountain and take photos...it was going to be epic.

We all decided that we should do it together, as a team, for moral and physical support should anybody decide to chicken out of the Antarctic plunge. With a 1, 2, 3.... we all start stripping off our layers and layers of clothing (one outer waterproof foul weather gear jacket, one thick down winter jacket, one long sleeve thermal, one inner tank top, one scarf, one wool hat, one pair of warm gloves, one pair of waterproof foul weather pants, one pair of semi waterproof ski pants, one pair of thermal underpants, one pair of warm sock liners, one pair of thick wool socks, and finally, one pair of waterproof gum boots) and ran into the water.

Our ideas of swimming laps, posing for pictures, splashing one another in slow motion quickly turned into: screaming into the water, dipping our bodies in and then screaming right back out, all the way until we got back to land. It wasn't so much of a "swim" as it was a "screaming mess of people plunging their bodies into melted ice cubes."

I have never felt such BITING cold before. The water was so cold that it felt like it was burning my skin. It was FREEZING. I don't think I could have lasted more than 40 seconds in that water without losing a few limbs.

What happened to the thermal springs? The hot water that we could bathe in and relax in? We felt DECEIVED. Now, we know the real reason why this island is called Deception Island. But we did it. We managed to voluntarily throw ourselves into some of the coldest waters in the world and live to tell the tale. We took the plunge. Literally.

If George had known that his life with me would take us to places like Antarctica and doing things like swimming in the Antarctic waters, I think he may have had second thoughts about taking "that other plunge" with me. But by this time, it was already too late: he had warned me not to fall in love with him; he forgot to warn himself not to fall in love with me.

Ⓙ

我們搭的船是研究船，上面有很多研究人員，我們有更多機會進去一般人不能去的地方。那天研究人員要數企鵝有幾隻、觀察牠們的變化。我跟 George 被分派到研究企鵝大便的工作，要看它的顏色，也要幫忙算企鵝數量、有多少隻是雙胞胎，但老實說真的數不出來，太多隻了，整區都是，而且企鵝笨笨的、容易跌倒還會亂動。

我們划獨木舟時，看到了許多鯨魚。當你看到水面上有很多泡泡，就知道鯨魚要出現了。如果你看到鯨魚的蹤影，又靠你很近，你絕不能從牠們面前經過，只能從後面。

那時當我們準備划回船上時，發現有鯨魚來了，牠們離我們非常近，突然間 George 開始慌張地叫著我的名字：「Janet, Janet, there is a whale…」，有隻鯨魚想要游上來水面，我們從牠的頭、尾巴、背部全都看得清清楚楚，那時我想完蛋了，我們可能要翻船了，因為牠的尾巴若一甩我們就會翻過去，當下我一直喊著：「Oh my God! Oh my God! Oh my God!」說時遲那時快，有一隻鯨魚跳出水面、接著第兩隻上來，還噴水把我們整身都弄濕了！我們真的很擔心會翻船，距離近到可以完全盯著牠的眼睛，又恐怖又好玩！我們有裝一個水底攝影機，雖然因為沒對到焦，完全沒拍到這個驚險的鏡頭，但卻錄到鯨魚在對話的聲音，很有趣！

我們結婚前晚在南極陸地露營，在那裡露營很特別要自己在雪地挖「床」，挖好後再鋪一層隔水的東西，最後塞進睡袋。本來我跟 George 要挖兩個可以一起睡的洞，但是他奶奶是希臘人比較傳統，要我們結婚前還是分開睡，所以我們最後還是一人挖一個洞「分床睡」。那晚我睡得很好，

可能因為我已經習慣外景，所以很容易睡。但 George 卻相反，因為他的睡袋漏水，又很擔心海豹，因為我們在睡袋裡的樣子有一點像海豹，George 很害怕海豹會過來「侵犯」他，或是企鵝跑過來他身上大便，緊張的他整夜都沒睡。

皮皮剉

by Janet

George 跟我個性南轅北轍。你也知道,我很愛冒險。George 就還好。所以,我得用三寸不爛之舌,說服他陪我到南極露營。錯過那晚,這輩子就甭想在南極大陸露營了,機會難得,怎能錯過。一生只有一次機會!

當然,前提是要說服 George。他不是個愛冒險的人,又喜歡住得舒舒服服的。露營鐵定不舒服。

1. George 最大的問題恐怕是:南極沒有廁所。老實說,南極規定很嚴,凡走過不可留下痕跡。人類排泄物也包括其中。當然也不能在冰雪中挖洞偷偷來了。換句話說,我們只能提一個水桶,當作男女共用的屎尿盆。基於某種「奇特」原因,George 很不願蹲在水桶前,把屁股暴露在全天下人面前。至於我,則覺得在一群企鵝旁邊上廁所也蠻有趣的。可能我是女生吧。我們就愛結伴上廁所。

2. 危險:在南極露營過夜,被海豹踐踏或攻擊的可能性微乎其微,但即使是萬分之一的機會,也足以讓 George 打退堂鼓。想在那露營,就要有跟海豹、企鵝、鼾聲如雷的同船旅伴共眠的打算。結果,海豹根本沒什麼好擔心的。雖說裹在繭一般的睡袋裡,確實看似呼呼大睡的海豹,但我想我們看起來應該沒性感到能吸引海豹上門、找我們「玩玩」。真正問題在於,海豹睡眠習慣與人類大不相同。有時到了三更半夜,他們會開始呼朋引伴,乍聽有點像夜店裡彈奏的貝斯聲。咚滋咚滋咚滋切切切切。George 三番兩次醒來,以為置身舞廳,過一陣子發現咚滋咚滋咚滋聲響愈來愈大,這才意會到,海豹距離我們愈來愈近,快把他嚇死了,於是,他沒能一夜好眠……

3. 自掘墳墓:在南極露營不是用帳篷。帶到陸上的東西要盡量精簡,以免留下太多人類的痕跡。所以要在陸上過夜的話,就得先自掘墳墓。長條形的方型冰洞,塞得下你和睡

袋就夠了。挖好冷冰冰的墳墓之後,要確保把底部拍平,免得床上有碎冰(否則,就算你的床墊再高檔舒適,也會像睡在健康步道上)。接著,塞入睡袋之前,把睡墊鋪在冰床上,即使只是薄薄一層,也有不錯的保暖防水效果。最後,則要塞入兩層睡袋:外層睡袋必須有防水功能,好阻絕雨雪、海豹的尿滲入內層睡袋。內層睡袋最好是厚羽絨材質,能防止體溫散去,有助於保暖。

4. 黑夜:南極到了夏天,可沒有黑夜這種東西。南極在地球底端,夏天(十二月至二月期間)基本上二十四小時都是白晝。我們去的時候,剛剛好是一月中旬,也就是說:夜晚不會天黑。待在船艙時,因有窗簾或捲簾可以放下來,不太會去注意。而如果是待在冰層上,半夜走出來,就會發現半夜看似凌晨五點……凌晨五點則看似晚間七點。

所以說,有鑑於上述因素,原以為 George 會提議我們在鏡頭前做做樣子,假裝在陸上

過夜,實際上再偷偷摸摸溜回船上去,享受一夜好眠,結果他竟然願意陪我到南極露營,著實讓我喜出望外。

幸運的是,有兩件事發生了。首先,充氣船都收回船上去了,要等到早上才會靠回陸地。所以,船員離開後,我們基本上就是擱淺在陸地上,更別想半夜起身摸回暖呼呼的被窩了。再者,George 的奶奶曾告訴他,結婚前夕不能與未婚妻同床。嗯,在南極雪堆裡各睡各的棺材,應該也算有守約吧?

光憑這點,就足以說服 George 陪我在南極大陸露營。也正因如此,我們在婚前之夜都「皮皮剉」了。

更新:
你或許好奇,我們後來到底睡得如何。我沒睡很久,頂多四個鐘頭左右,卻可說是我這輩子睡得最沉的一次。我當時累得精疲力竭,一爬進睡袋,覺得自己就像窩在毛茸茸

睡袋裡的嬰兒，立刻備感溫暖安全，倒頭就
睡。後來會醒來，是因為有一丁點冰水和冷
風鑽進外層睡袋。

至於 George 睡得如何，就由他自己說吧。
（J）

Janet Hsieh

Getting Cold Feet

by Janet

George and I are very different. I love adventure as you know. George, not so much. Somehow, I managed to convince him that we needed to go camping in Antarctica. It was the only night that they were going to make camping on the Antarctic continent possible, and there's no way that I was going to give up that chance. It's a once in a lifetime opportunity!

Of course, I had to convince George first. Not only does he usually not like adventure, he also doesn't like to be uncomfortable. And we were in for a night of discomfort.

1. Probably George's biggest issue: there is no toilet on Antarctica. In fact, the rules are so strict that you can't leave anything on Antarctica. And that includes human waste. So, we couldn't dig a hole and bury our business in the snow and ice. That means that there was just one bucket which served as our communal bucket-o-pee/poo for both girls and boys. George, for some *strange* reason, usually doesn't like to have his rear end hanging out for all the world to see as he squats over a bucket. I on the other hand, think it would be kinda fun to go to the bathroom next to penguins also doing their business. Maybe it's a girl thing - we like going to the bathroom together.

2. Danger: While the likelihood of getting trampled or attacked by a seal is very very low, the fact that it's something that could even possibly happen, is enough to turn George off the idea of camping overnight in Antarctica. We were going to be sleeping next to seals, penguins, and snoring shipmates. Turns out the seals really weren't anything to be worried about. Even though we looked suspiciously like sleeping seals ourselves in our cocoon sleeping bags, I guess we weren't sexy looking enough to attract any seals to come over and try and "play" with us. However, seals don't have the same sleeping patterns as humans apparently. Sometime, in the middle of the night, they started to call to one another and it sounded a little bit like the bass in a nightclub: don-che-dong-che-dong-che-un-che-un-che. George kept waking up thinking that he was in a dance club somewhere only to realize that the 'don-che-dong-che-dong-che' was actually getting louder, which meant that the seals were really close to us, which meant that he was freaking out, which meant that, he didn't get a good night's rest...

3. Digging our own coffins: When you camp in Antarctica, you don't use tents. We want to minimize the amount of stuff that we bring onto land so that we don't leave too many prints or human traces. So in order to sleep, you first have to dig your own grave. A long rectangular ice pit just large enough for you to fit in it with your sleeping bag. Once you've dug your icy grave, then you want to make sure the bottom of it is flat and patted down so you don't get any ice chunks in your bed (that would be like sleeping with huge rocks in your posturepedic mattress). Then, you lay your sleeping mat on the bottom to provide you with one thin layer of warmth and waterproof protection underneath your sleeping bag. After that, you use two layers of bags: an outer sleeping bag which is waterproof and keeps the snow, rain, and seal pee from dripping onto your inner layer. Your inner sleeping bag should be a nice thick down sleeping sac which reflects your body heat onto itself and keeps you warm.

4. Lights out: in Antarctica - during the Summer months - there's no such thing. Antarctica is so low on the globe that it's basically 24 hours of daylight during Summer (which is December - February). We were smack in the middle of January, which meant: no darkness during the night. In our cabins on the ship, you don't notice the lack of darkness so much because we have curtains and shades to pull down. But when you are out in the middle of the ice, midnight feels like 5am...which at the same time feels like 7pm.

So, given all of these things, I was very surprised that George agreed to go camping in Antarctica. I thought he would suggest that we just pretend to sleep there overnight for the camera, but in reality secretly sneak onto the ship and get a good night's rest.

Luckily for me though, two things happened. One: all of the zodiacs were going back to the ship and wouldn't come back to land until the morning. So, we were pretty much stranded on land once the crew left: there was no getting up in the middle of the night to sneak into our warm comfy beds. And two: George's grandma had once told him that we were supposed to sleep in separate beds the night before the wedding. Well, sleeping in two separate coffins in the Antarctic snow must count, right?

With this, I was able to convince George to camp

with me on the Antarctic continent and that's how we both got "cold feet" the night before our wedding day.

UPDATE:

In case you were wondering how we slept: I didn't get much sleep - only about four hours or so, but those four hours were some of the best sleep I've ever had. I was exhausted, crawled into my sleeping bag and immediately felt warm and safe, crashed like a baby in a feather cocoon and then only woke up because I had a little bit of cold water and air coming in through my outer sleeping bag.

As for George - I'll let him tell you how well he slept.

Ⓙ

Janet Hsieh

George 怎麼看「皮皮剉」這件事
Getting Cold Feet: George's Response

by George

簡直噩夢。在南極露營過夜，是我這輩子睡過最糟的一場覺。

首先：那可是婚前最後一夜。是你人生當中非常重要的日子。

不——首先：你人在南極。

不不——首先最重要的是：你可是睡在薄薄冰雪砌成的墳墓裡，下方可是南極冰塊。

喔不——首先尤其重要的是：南極夏天沒有晚上這一回事。而要掩蓋這個事實，你得把自己包在「被套」（也就是防水被單，完完全全包覆著你，以拉鏈封口）裡，三更半夜聽那層薄薄的布料不停被雨雪淅瀝拍打。又或許，如果你跟我一樣無敵幸運，防水被單封得很密，那麼亮晃晃的夜裡，只會有一些些雨雪滲到你臉上。

言而總之，其中最大的錯誤，就是打從一開始，選擇在這地球上數一數二不適宜人居的鬼地方露營。

我推薦大家都來試試。Ⓖ

It was horrible. Spending the night camping in Antarctica. Worst night of sleep in my life.

First of all: it's the night before your wedding. One of the biggest days of your life.

No - first of all: you're in Antarctica.

No no - first of all: you're in a shallow grave of snow and ice on some ice mass in Antarctica.

NO - first of all, there's no nighttime during the Antarctic Summer. To cover up that fact, your "duvet cover" (also known as a was a waterproof sheet that completely envelops you and is secured by a zipper) - will be lightly tapped upon throughout the night as the snow and rain falls upon the thin material. And perhaps - if you're exceptionally fortunate like I was - your waterproof casing would close only just enough to ensure at least some of that snow and rainfall would be allowed onto your face during the light-filled evening.

One of the above is the start of the experience that is camping in one of the most inhospitable continents on the planet.

I would recommend the experience to everyone. Ⓖ

結婚當天,我在化妝的同時請助理去勘
景,因為我想要有企鵝在旁邊的地點,還
要有很白很乾淨的環境。這時我也請所有
朋友準備著裝,因為我們隨時會開始!我
事前還拜託朋友不要穿運動禦寒外套來南
極,希望他們穿正式的西裝跟洋裝,而朋
友們也很認真地準備了。

我們當天才臨時準備結婚誓詞，因為前幾天都太放鬆了，一直到當天才想起要寫。我跟 George 不想讓對方知道自己寫什麼，因為我們都想創造驚喜，但又想確定彼此的篇幅長度可以 match。最後我們分別拿給證婚人看，他說 ok 不用改很 match！

在證婚人致詞、雙方家長講致詞後，接下來就換我們各自講婚禮誓詞。這段婚禮誓詞是半開玩笑半正式的，過程中有哭有笑卻又很感人。我們整個婚禮過程才 15 分鐘，因為我本來就不希望婚禮太冗長，也沒有特別計畫要怎樣的婚禮，但完成之後反而覺得很完美，因為我們不想要太多附加的花、蠟燭、細節⋯⋯只希望以冰山為背景、企鵝作花童，這樣是難以取代的。

我覺得自己很幸運，那天雖然零度但是沒有風，要是溫度比較高但有風反而會比較冷。後來婚禮完成也拍完照片後竟開始下雨跟雪，真是 timing 剛剛好。

Chapter. 07

相信愛情
Trust in Love

與 George 第一次見面的那天，我就出了一連串的糗，那晚我生病、心血來潮地抽了水煙（我根本不抽煙的，為什麼那天會抽水煙？真是猜不透）、然後昏倒。我們兩個對那晚的記憶，還有漸漸變好朋友的那些時刻的細節，根本就都有很大的出入！

也許我們其中一方的記性不好，但我們絕對不是不珍惜記憶，而是我們註定要為這件事一起爭執到老！

愛情與現實的角力？

那晚後過了大概十年，兩個人開始交往之後不久，我就意識到自己已瘋狂愛上 George，而且我想要永遠跟他在一起！這種感覺，我以前也從未經歷過，如果以前跟我說世界上有這樣的愛情，我可能還不相信。但它就這樣發生了，而我也明白這種感覺了。

以前我也曾經愛上別人，但是在真正投入與做出任何形式的承諾之前，都會經過一段時間的試探、角力以及要不要全心投入的掙扎。但是對 George 完全沒有這個階段。從交往到深深感覺到想跟他在一起一輩子，這之間沒有什麼思考的轉折，我根本就隨時願意跟他遠走高飛！

當然冷靜下來之後，一段關係一定有一些與現實的角力，在我們的例子裡，與其對「婚姻」本身有什麼焦慮，比如說害怕妥協等等，我們兩個人更苦惱的是如何在事業與愛情當中做出安排──尤其是我們的工作帶著我們各自在全世界東奔西跑。多年來的相處，我們親眼目睹對方為了事業，付出很大的心力，因此誰也沒想過要求對方放棄事業，與自己團聚，但是我們也深知如果一直這樣下去，也可能在路途中失去對方。因此要如何將這樣的兩個人

納入一幅共同的未來圖像，是我們永無止盡的話題。

未來我會希望能夠將工作集中在更大的時間區塊裡，而不是分布在一年四季，時時都在工作，只能用零碎的時間去找 George。原本這次的結婚之旅，我們有討論到也許 George 也可以試試看當個外景主持人，後來我們都發現這個工作並不是他真正嚮往的。

不過，在這些永無止盡的討論裡，我們談了更多事情，因為我們現在是朋友兼戀人兼家人了，什麼都能聊，聊的還比以前更多；很嚴肅的時候可以聊金錢、死亡、分手、愛上別人；我們希望為對方好好地活著，但是也期許自己未來萬一不能在一起，也會祝福。而很輕鬆的時候，我們也可以故意吊對方胃口，讓對方吃醋，比如說他會假裝有女生要約他，而當我夏天去法國的時候，他還會故作輕鬆狀地問我：

有沒有去前男友住的城市逛逛啊？

這樣看似輕鬆的玩笑與遊戲，背後是尊重與堅信對方，未來也會帶領著我們度過更多考驗！

曾經的未來愛情想像，與往日愛情

我小時候覺得自己會結婚，生五個小孩，George 則是想像他會跟一個叫 Sarah 的女生結婚哈哈！一路上我們都曾經跟別人交往，我曾經覺得可以為法國前男朋友拋棄一切自我也沒關係，而 George 也曾經是一個自信心過剩的人，無論是人生或者是談戀愛的時候。

我們剛認識的時候都還在摸索人生的方向，那時我們都面臨著來自父母的壓力——原本他念法，我念醫，對父母來

說，好好的醫生律師不當，卻突然轉往完全不相關的跑道，而我們相對也會承受一些壓力；除此之外，當時我們這麼年輕，還沒有準備好談戀愛。

George 說過，如果我們當初一認識就開始交往，我們不會懂得欣賞自己已經擁有的，人生的重點也會擺在別的事情上面，或者根本是還看不清楚生命將走到何方。如果沒有生命經驗的堆積，還有沒有前面幾段感情讓我們學習，我們就會少發現很多關於自己的事情，也就不會有現在的成熟與智慧，來迎接對方的到來。
頭也不回地投入了

這次五十幾天的旅行兼工作，讓我們可以住在一起生活與工作近兩個月。遠距離戀愛從來沒有讓我們感到害怕惶恐——因為我們一直都是遠距離的關係。一起生活與工作近兩個月，才是全新的經驗，這是一趟非常緊湊與密集的工作兼旅程，我們幾乎沒有獨自相處的閒暇時間，卻又緊密生活在一起這麼長的時間，這還是第一次。

其實這整趟旅行都像是對我們關係的一種比喻，除了史詩般橫跨三洲的大遷徙之外——還脫衣服跳進原本以為是溫泉、結果是全世界最冷的水裡，無論是出自無知或勇氣，我們頭也不回，就這麼跳進這冰冷的水裡（嗯？說好的溫泉呢？）。這大概就像我毫無預警地愛上了相識十多年的 George，然後再義無反顧地，我們兩個人投身婚姻裡吧！

水是冰冷的，我們的未來是未知的謎團，可是經過這一次的旅行，我們更加確信要組成家庭的信念，我們的關係是越來越溫暖與緊密的。無論如何，在這旅程的最後，我們結婚了，就算知道人不見得能如願永遠在一起，但是我們都希望未來的圖像裡有彼此……並且一輩子爭執我們相識那晚的真相！

摸黑行進

by George

意料之外的，我們無法預知，只能走一步算一步。未來，就像一個黑暗至極的房間，往往讓人卻步，腳步再小心，都難保不會撞到東西，傷到自己。

Janet 跟我是十年前認識的，當時我們才二十出頭，都還在摸索將來要做什麼。對於人生規劃，都有來自父母的壓力，而我們真正想做的，也都與父母的期待背道而馳。這些共通點確實把我們拉近，但時機還不對。

我在想，就算 Janet 和我那時就交往，畢竟人生還有其他追求，恐怕也不會懂得珍惜。又或者，我們會因此放棄理想。在房裡摸黑前進，有個人可以牽手固然很好，但我相信，與其互相牽制、左顧右盼，不如保持友好關係，各自走在不同人生跑道上，對我們才是更好的選擇。

要是我們早就在一起，我也許就沒有衝勁前往新加坡，遑論要在說英語的亞洲國家打下一片市場了。而對 Janet 來說，她或許會被我說動，陪我回英國讀法律，這麼一來，就失去在台灣大紅大紫的機會了。

過去由於人生規劃不同，我們幾乎都在世界各地工作，現在即使工作關係也需要東奔西跑，也不會令我們漸行漸遠。Janet 和我都很習慣維繫遠距離感情，交往以來，多半時候都相隔數千哩，而且都為期頗長一段時間，但都會保持聯繫。所以，遠距離嚇不到我們。

現在，我們會盡量協調工作時間，避免老是相隔兩地。以現階段來說，如果要有小孩，勢必要做些改變。這也是為什麼，踏上這段旅程，一起走過德州、阿根廷、南極，是件很棒的事：我們能長時間待在同一個地方，而且不單是每天生活在一塊，而是工作在一塊。除了夜幕降臨要睡覺之外——雖說南極沒有夜幕這回事——我們

可是連續五十天都膩在一塊。

我們共同的未來，就像這趟德州、阿根廷、南極之旅一樣，十成八九都充滿驚險與挑戰。旅途中要探索未知（尤其對我這樣旅遊經驗較少的人來說）、馬不停蹄遷徙、面對滿檔行程，時常讓人疲於奔命，但好在我們是堅強的一對。最後，我們還是結婚了。 Ⓖ

Walking in the Dark

by George

You can't foresee the unexpected - we deal with each moment as they come along. The future is like a very dark room: it's scary to venture into most of the time, and no matter how cautiously you proceed, you'll bump into things and hurt yourself every so often.

Janet and I first met over 10 years ago - when we were in our early 20s. At that point, both of us were still figuring out what we were going to do with our lives. We both had pressure from our parents to go one way, whilst we both felt we wanted to go another. And whilst we both bonded over those similarities, we both weren't ready for a relationship.

I think if Janet and I started dating back then, we wouldn't have appreciated what we had; we'd be too focused on other things. Or perhaps we would've lost sight of where we wanted to go with our lives. As much as it would've been nice to have someone's hand to hold in that dark room, I think we were better off finding each other along our own separate paths, rather than perhaps pulling and tugging each other each time we wanted to explore a different direction.

If we were dating earlier, I perhaps wouldn't have had the drive to go to Singapore, where I found a lot of work there in the English speaking Asian market; perhaps Janet - rather than staying in Taiwan and getting her big break out there - would've been convinced to come to England with me when I was there studying law.

Now - because of our separate experiences that have allowed us to work around the world, even when our paths took us (and still take us) to separate corners of Earth, it doesn't phase us. Janet and I are used to being in a long-distance relationship; most of our relationship has been about staying connected despite being thousands of miles apart from each other for extended periods of time. Long-distances don't scare us.

Lately, we've been discussing how to manage our careers and our time so that we're in the same part of the world more often. We're coming to a time in our relationship where - if we want to start a family of our own - we're going to need to make some changes. That's why it was nice to embark on this journey through Texas, Argentina and Antarctica together: we spent a lot of time in the same location, not only

living together every day, but working together too - for fifty days non-stop, save for the occasional nap when it was dark. And there were times in Antarctica when it never got dark.

Much like what all of our collective future shall and often will be: our journey through Texas, Argentina and Antarctica was pretty scary and challenging. The journey into unknown territory (especially for me: the less travelled of the two), the constant journeying, and relentless film schedule were all very tiring at times, but we're both a stronger couple for it. We got married at the end of it after all. Ⓖ

George Young

南極不是屬於任何國家的,大家只能在這裡設科學站。我們參觀的科學站就是當初發現臭氧層破洞的地方。這個烏克蘭科學站以前是英國的,英國人在裡頭建了一個酒吧,所以這裡是全世界最南端的酒吧!

通常去南極的人大部分都是退休有一點年紀的,很少年輕人去,所以我們一行四十幾個人不僅都很年輕,還有幾個打扮很辣的女性好朋友,進去時他們很興奮,大家一起喝酒、跳舞,玩得好 high。那個酒吧有個傳統,如果女生現場捐內衣,他就送你一杯免費調酒,我也捐了我的給他們。這時 George 生氣地說,為什麼只有女生有!我也要捐內褲! Bartender 開玩笑說:「你這樣要付雙倍的錢喔!」哈哈!

我們很幸運，本來要選南極一個教堂結
婚，但經過教堂時發現天氣很糟、風很大，
所以決定換地方也改變行程。有另外一艘
船繼續走原本的行程，我們在回程途中又
碰到它，沒想到他們說整整六天航行都在
下雪下雨，也就是說如果我們選擇這個行
程就會經歷很糟的天氣。但相對的，我們
後來航行幾乎都很晴朗、景色也很美。果
然當地人說「Weather Changes on a dime.」
天氣在一瞬間就會改變，早上可能萬里無
雲，下午馬上狂風暴雨。

我跟 George 本來就不想舉辦太麻煩的婚禮，一開始想登記就好了，卻因為一連串巧合跑出這個計畫。原本我們以為只有五、六個朋友會跟我們去，沒想到一放出消息卻有很多人想去，計劃越來越大，加上節目製作人也想去，想順便拍點東西回來，後來索性規畫成完整的節目，變成一個五十天、五十個人的行程。這次真的很感謝大家，推掉好多各自的工作，陪我們完成這趟充滿紀念價值的愛之旅！

勇氣的意義，對我來說，會隨著年紀而改變。

by Janet

對小時候的我來說，勇氣是三年級時，放膽走到暗戀對象的座位，偷他的便當。我可是想方設法，才沒被他跟老師發現（話說此人後來竟然出櫃了，還跟一個超帥的男人結婚……要是時光能倒轉，我一定勸當時九歲的我去偷別人的便當）。

接著到了國中，勇氣成了對抗權威（譬如老師或父母），極力爭取我認為不可剝奪的生存權益。你也知道，像是去看限制級電影，不讓爸媽陪同；或吵著買很潮的同學都有的五十九美元鞋子（只有我沒有）；或吵著要養小狗，雖然牠會在客廳地毯上尿尿，但我保證會好好教牠，愛牠一輩子……你也知道，這些對當時的我來說，簡直跟生死同樣重要。

後來讀了高中，勇氣變得比較內斂了：是放在心裡的那種。那時我跟初戀男友分手，需要好大勇氣才放得下，接受現實：我不是他的天命真女，我們不會結婚，不會有五個孩子，之後就算他交了新女友，我也得眼睜睜看他們手牽手，不再心碎。

大學就難熬了。非常難熬。生平第一個好友車禍身亡，我必須鼓足勇氣，才有辦法接受這個噩耗。傷心欲絕的我，費好大把勁才爬出低谷，認清死亡是人生必經過程，而這輩子結交過這麼棒的朋友，儘管時間不長，也該感到慶幸了。年紀輕輕，就得和朋友說再見，直到現在，我仍不知自己那時是怎麼辦到的。但我確實做到了。還學到一件事：說再見，不代表你會忘卻這個人。

畢業後，最勇敢的一刻，恐怕就是放棄醫學院，改行做模特兒了。我意思是說，一般人不會幹這種傻事吧？當醫生一向是我的夢想，讀了四年大學，一連數月準備考試、趕考、面試，好不容易進了醫學院，結果我竟然輟學，搬回台灣當模特兒。這需要勇氣。很大很大的勇氣。吃東西可是我畢生最大樂

趣。偏偏模特兒不能大吃特吃。我要不是吃了熊心豹子膽，就是徹底瘋了。也許兩者都有一點。

然而，當初若沒碰到這些關鍵時刻，要是我沒鼓起勇氣，下這些決定，就沒有現在的我了。

勇氣簡單來說，就是無懼無恐，或者那兩粒很大（西班牙語用「那兩粒」形容一個人「勇氣可嘉」）。這種能力，讓人膽敢躍下飛機，從五層樓高的懸崖跳水，在一群橫衝直撞的公牛前方奔跑，把頭伸進鱷魚嘴裡，或與鯊魚共泳。以這層意思來看，我那兩粒可大呢（我倒不介意這麼說自己）。這些我還真的不怕，反而令我躍躍欲試！我很喜歡這種腎上腺素飆高的感覺。注視鯊魚的眼睛，或者俯視數千公尺下、小得像痘痘的車輛時，我確實會緊張，心臟咚咚地跳，但即便知道有潛在危險，我還是會踏出一步，挑戰未知。

反觀 George 這個人，簡直跟我南轅北轍。凡是有潛在危險或可怕的事，他一蓋不愛。碰到懸崖，他恨不得離得遠遠的。寧可赤手空拳勇闖賊窩，對抗持刀壞蛋，拯救他一生摯愛……在電動裡……也不願冒著斷手斷腳的風險，瘋狂一下。嗯，很好。

怪的是，這樣的我們最後竟然會在一起。充滿異國情調的未知國度，讓我心癢難耐；對George 來說，大概只有手臂上被蚊子咬的地方會癢得讓他想抓抓。我渴望冒險，是個無可救藥的行動派；他則熱衷最新上市的 3C產品。我為腎上腺素飆升而生；George 則是……嗯，為生活而生。

我們能處得這麼好，總能說服對方嘗鮮，說來也真是奇蹟。有一次，我成功說服 George陪我參加為期十天、航向大西洋島國東加的帆船行。有一次，George 說服我，跟他飛到舊金山，四處閒晃，啥也不做。我要他陪我到德州騎馬，後來在阿根廷又騎了一次。我

也在他說服下，去德州馬法鎮看 PRADA 裝置藝術。

很多人說，我比 George「勇敢」，但他在二〇一五年一月二十六日說的一席話，讓我感動得熱淚盈眶。應該說，在場者全都熱淚盈眶。它讓我見識到，所謂勇敢，遠遠不只是冒險的本領或渴望。

那天，George 在我們婚禮上，當著四十八名來賓和二千三百零四隻企鵝的面發言，以下原文照錄：

「現實生活中，我往往會避開令我害怕的事。但跟妳在一起，妳總是讓我做些瘋狂的事，就像我們正在做的這件事，還是在這種地方。當初我提議南極，純粹是開玩笑，妳卻當真了。人一生中，有幾件事特別恐怖，跟人告白就是其中一種。是妳讓我辦到了……。是妳讓我辦到的，但不是因為妳說了什麼，而是因為，妳就是妳。」

就是這席話，無論我這輩子有過幾次冒險之舉，我都甘敗下風。George 讓我見識到，什麼是勇氣。把自己百分百交付給對方，無條件愛著對方，朋友啊，這需要勇氣。所以，就算不想承認，也不得不說，George 那兩粒贏過我了。①

Definition of Courage

by Janet

At first, courage was having the guts to go up to the guy that I had a crush on in 3rd grade and steal his lunch box. I don't know which part was harder - not getting noticed by the teachers or not getting noticed by him (who by the way, later came out of the closet and married a very handsome man... if only there was a way to go back in time and tell my 9 year old self to steal somebody else's lunch box.)

Then, in middle school, courage became standing up to authority (such as a teacher or parent) and fighting for what, at the time, I believed was crucial for my very existence. You know, things like being able to go watch an R rated movie WITHOUT parental guidance, or letting me buy those $59 shoes which every single cool kid (except for me) had, or letting me keep the puppy which had just peed on the living room rug, but which I would personally train and love forever and ever and ever.... you know, those type of life or death things.

High school came around and courage became more internal: right in the heart. It took courage to get over my first boyfriend and being able to accept that I was not the love of his life, we weren't going to get married and have 5 kids, and I was just going to have to be comfortable watching him hold hands with his new girlfriend.

College was a tough one. Really tough. Then, I had to build up the courage to face the loss of my first friend to a car accident. I had to dig myself out of my sadness and accept the fact that death was a part of life and at least I was lucky enough to have had such a good friend in my life at all, no matter how short of a time it was. To this day, I don't know how I managed to have the courage to be able to say goodbye to a friend taken from us way too early. But I did. And I learned that saying goodbye doesn't mean you forget.

After graduating, my most courageous moment was probably when I gave up medical school to pursue a career in modeling. I mean, who DOES that, right? I had always wanted to be a doctor and it took me four years of college, several months of test preparation, exams, applications, and interviews to be accepted into medical school. And with one fell swoop (definition of "fell swoop": suddenly, in a single action. Origin: no idea. Good question!), I dropped out of medical school and moved back to Taiwan to be a model. This took courage. A lot. I mean, two of my favorite things in the world are eating and eating. And models don't eat. I was either courageous or insane. Maybe a little bit of both.

But without courage and without making all of these decisions and little moments in life that test your courage, I wouldn't be who I am today.

On the outside, courage can easily be categorized as lack of fear or having big cojones (Spanish for "big balls"). It's the ability to jump out of a plane, dive off of a five story cliff, run in front of charging bulls, sticking your head in a crocodile's head, or swimming with sharks. If this is the case, then I have pretty large cojones, if I don't mind saying so myself. I don't really fear these things - in fact, they excite me! I look forward to the adrenaline rush. And while yes, I do get nervous and my heart pounds as you look into the eyes of a shark or look down at the cars thousands of meters below which look like pimples they're so small, you're still able to take the step and face a potentially dangerous situation.

George, on the other hand, is very different. He does NOT like anything potentially dangerous or scary. He prefers to live his life far far far away from the edge. He'd rather fist fight his way through a crowd and save the love of his life from knife-wielding gangsters…. in a video game…than actually do anything insane that has the risk of limb-loss. Fair enough.

It is very strange that the both of us could ever end up together. I itch for travel to exotic and unknown locations. George will occasionally scratch the mosquito bites on his arm. I crave adventure and action. He craves the newest gadget that's just been launched. I live for adrenaline rushes. George lives for, well, life.

It is a wonder that we get along so well and that we always manage to convince each other to try out new things. I once convinced George to join me on a 10-day sailing trip to Tonga. And George convinced me to fly to San Francisco and just do nothing but hang out. I got George to ride a horse with me in Texas and then again in Argentina. He convinced me to go visit the Prada art installation in Marfa, Texas.

Most people would say I'm more "courageous" than

George. But he said something on January 26th, 2015 that brought me to tears. Brought everybody to tears actually. And showed me that there's so much more to courage than just a knack or desire for danger.

This is, word for word, what George said on our wedding day, in front of 48 guests and 2304 penguins:

"In my real life, I often avoid things that scare me. but not when I'm with you. You make me do some crazy stuff, including what we're doing now and where we're doing it. I was kind of kidding when I suggested Antarctica but you just ran with it. One of the scariest things you can do though, is to tell someone that you love them first. You made me do that...you made me do that not with words, but by being who you are."

With these words, George has outdone any physical activity I could have ever done in my past. He really showed me what it meant to be courageous. To give yourself 100% to somebody, to love them unconditionally. That, my friend, takes courage. So, as much as I don't like to admit it, George has bigger cojones than me. Ⓙ

回到熟悉的現實生活

by George

置身在地球最偏遠角落，許多事都很有新鮮感，上網難如登天就是其中一項。成群年輕人跟大人與世隔絕，那種感覺實在棒透了。有種煥然一新之感：倍覺新鮮之外，又有股懷舊感。船上除了最小的成員之外，其餘都曾活在沒有網路的世界，不過，我們大家的餘生恐怕都難逃它的魔掌了。

我們過了整整十一天幾乎沒有網路、智慧裝置的日子，唯一勉強算得上的，只有基本到不行的電子郵件（雖說是電子郵件，也是九〇年代、長度格式有限制的那種）。我們很多人都索性把手機、筆電、平板、智慧手錶擺在一旁，抬起頭來，和身邊的人談天、說悄悄話，或甚至跟遠處的人大聲呼喊。彷彿回到一去不復返的孩提時光，對世間紛擾一無所知的純真狀態。

我是不折不扣的3C迷，從醒來的一刻起，直到不得不闔眼入睡（有時甚至會刻意熬夜），我都倚賴網路為一切的知識泉源。因此，對於能來到南極，暫時與它被迫分離，尤其感到莫名感激。果然，無知就是福，儘管只有短短幾天也好。

南極的景致是這般引人入勝，不論有沒有網路，當低頭族都太浪費了，但我深信，起碼在船上，一定很多人會賴在餐廳或船艙，埋頭滑手機，不跟置身同空間的人交流。我覺得自己肯定也會犯同樣的錯。

一回到烏斯懷亞，大家第一件事就是登入社群網站，查看動態消息。像 Janet 跟我就立刻上傳一張合照，背景有「我們結婚了」的拉旗，接著便跨越時空國界與友人重拾聯繫。這種感覺，就像原本自以為不餓，結果一走進餐廳，聞到食物香味，看到菜單，立即變得飢腸轆轆。一重回網路的懷抱，與世隔絕的新鮮感隨即給拋到九霄雲外去了。

Janet 離開南極後，一直悵然若失，我倒不會。在那裡的時光，分分秒秒我都很享受，但現代人的生活方式我同樣熱愛。但話說回來，選擇上不上網是很幸福的一件事，兩者共存、任君選擇，更是完美不過了。

南極生活確實獨一無二，就像身在遺世獨立的桃花源一樣，尤其欣慰的是：那裡的網路爛透了。 Ⓖ

George Young

Back to Life as We Know It

by George

One of the most refreshing things about being on one of the most remote parts of the planet was that the internet was hard to come by. A bunch of adults and young adults were disconnected from the rest of the Earth, and it felt great. It felt refreshing: at the same time new and nostalgic. All of us, apart from the youngest on the ship, had grown up with at least part of their lives in the pre-internet world, and all of us will no doubt live out the remaining years we have completely connected to it.

We had eleven days separated from the internet and smart devices for all but the most basic of emails (and even said emails were limited to 1990s-style restrictions in length and format). Most of us simply put our phones and laptops and tablets and smartwatches away, lifted our heads up, and communicated to those that were in talking, shouting or whispering distance. We all played as children from an era that we'll likely never see again, and with the same child-like obliviousness to the goings on in rest of the world.

I'm a huge techy, and the internet is the apple of knowledge from which I eagerly bite - from the moment I wake, to the time that I absolutely need to sleep (and sometimes after that period has passed). It's therefore especially strange for me to be so grateful for Antarctica granting me the time away from it. Ignorance is bliss indeed, at least for a short while.

I'm sure the beauty of the place would have dragged us away from the small screen, internet or no, but I am positive that - within the ship at least - there'd be a lot more of our number simply sitting at the dinner table or cabin hunched over our phones instead of socialising with those who share the same immediate oxygen. I know I certainly would have been guilty of that.

Once we were back in Ushuaia, one of the first things we all did was check our various social media accounts, and newsfeeds. Janet and I posted a picture of us with the "Just Married" wedding banner, and generally we communicated through space and beyond borders once more. Much like those moments where you didn't think you were hungry until you walked into the restaurant, smelled the food and saw the menu: I didn't miss the lack of internet until it surrounded and enveloped me once again.

I didn't feel the same sadness that Janet felt post-Antarctica. I loved every moment of the place, but I also appreciate the modern world that we live in. I love the fact that we have both, and it would be very nice indeed if we could keep both intact.

Antarctica is certainly an experience unlike any other - it's a different world within our world, and thankfully: the internet sucks over there. Ⓖ

George Young

Chapter. 08

下一個遠方
Beyond the End

未曾參與的二十幾年

我們兩個人的人生,都有二十年的過去是
彼此沒有參與到的,也因為我們從不同的
地方走到一起,才能夠長出新的自己。

George 在英國長大,他來自多元種族的
家庭──父母親各是馬來西亞華人與希臘
人。他的家裡總共有四兄弟,有兩位是自
閉症者,四兄弟全部都是讀英國的私立學
校,與我的家庭背景截然不同。我的爸媽
都是台灣人,爸爸對當時的社會沒有言論
自由的狀況相當不滿,於是與媽媽結婚之
後,兩個人就離開台灣,先到了夏威夷,
後來在美國德州落腳。所以我們長大的地
方非常不同,生活方式、甚至是說話的方
式(雖然都是講泛稱為英文的語言),都
有很大的差異。當然,相對來說,其實大
家透過美國的電視影集都對美國文化有很
多認識,至少第一次去到美國的人都不至
於太驚訝,George 也是一樣,他小時候看

很多很多美國影集,但我對英國文化只有
一些基本的認識而已。

我們喜歡彼此來自很不同的地方,喜歡彼
此是這麼不同的人;我喜歡他是個跟我個
性截然不同,卻心胸非常開闊的人。因此
我們都會對彼此的生活脈絡有很多好奇,
都想看看對方的生長環境;在這次的結婚
旅程之前他就來過我長大的地方,他覺得
那裡非常美國,跟他小時候看影集的印象
差不多。我也去逛過他的學校,也認識了
他所有的朋友,都是人生不同階段認識的
朋友們。喔我還記得一件很好笑的事,就
是去南極前我為了給他驚喜,自己偷偷跑
到倫敦,他那時在新加坡,我們之間有八
小時的時差我卻要假裝還在同一個時區的
台灣,這個驚喜實在騙得我很辛苦。這個
驚喜的結尾就是我找了他很多好朋友,拍
了一段他們一起狂歡還請了脫衣舞孃來家
裡的影片──而這個脫衣舞孃就是我哈
哈!

以及在一起的往後二十年

Ⓖ 二十年之後的生活喔……我們會養一條機器狗，坐在 3D 列印的沙發上，抱怨我們女兒 Janeorge 聽的音樂有夠快、有夠吵，偶爾還會聊起以前爸爸媽媽都要用電源線將手機電池充電呢，那真的是好遙遠的事啊。

Ⓙ 雖然兩個人都很忙，而且都還相隔很遠，但是我們兩個都很喜歡小孩子，所以完全不排斥有小孩。其實我小時候想像自己未來有大概五個小孩吧哈哈哈哈！二十年後我五十幾歲，小孩子已經在讀中學了。我們兩個那時大概會是在一起聊一些很無聊很好笑的事情。

Ⓖ 我一直在想……以後我們當了父母，情況一定是我管東管西，耳提面命這個要小心、那個不要碰，而 Janet 就是那種「哎呀有什麼關係呢？」的媽媽。

Ⓙ 但我覺得我們家一定會很好笑，無論瘋瘋癲癲還是一本正經的樣子，大家一定都很好笑。

Ⓖ 一段關係中總是要有兩種人，這樣才有意思，父母也要很不一樣才好玩。

Ⓙ 其實以前越開始衝刺事業的時候越覺得不可能有小孩，這麼艱鉅的事我辦不到。我看到很多朋友有了小孩之後生活有了劇烈的轉變，但我不想要生活有這麼多轉變，小時候有大家庭的想法就往後擺了。但是現在這個想法又重新回來啦，我會想要有三、四個小孩，熱熱鬧鬧的。但同時我又熱愛工作……

Ⓖ 確實，我們各自如何安排事業，會直接影響到生小孩的事情。但終究我們兩個都了解了──沒有任何一個人是「準備」好要迎接孩子的到來的，只有在兩個人關係很堅固的時候，才是迎接孩子到來的時機。

Ｊ 就像我朋友說的，我們兩個還是兩條線，有的時候還不小心往遠離對方的方向岔出去，小孩是連結我們的機會，不管我們的線走到哪，都會將我們緊緊牽牢。

預約下一個遠方

我們已經準備好要一起看世界了！這個世界也許是空間上的世界——美國、台灣、英國、新加坡、古巴……，也可以是情感的世界。

我們現在還一直在尋找在一起定居的可能性，現在列出來的地方是洛杉機、台灣、新加坡、倫敦、亞特蘭大，目前都沒有一個地方勝出，每個地方的順位隨著我們的事業狀態與選擇標準而一直浮動——如果要便利，台灣一定是第一順位，治安的話也許是新加坡吧，而說到國際文化中繼站，那就是選擇倫敦，George 的工作的話就是洛杉機……總之一直是浮動的狀態，目前我們完全沒有一個定論，因為我們的足跡與累積的事物就是散落在這麼多地方。

我們常常在討論：也許有一天走著走著，我們兩個就散了。二十年後，我們還為在一起嗎？會不會愛上別人，或者對彼此沒有感覺了？會一樣相愛但不再有吸引力

嗎？我們會將自己許多的想像都坦白地講出來，討論了很多未來的可能性，包含分離；我們有心理準備也許不會永遠在一起，孩子一上大學說不定我們就決定分開了。我們從朋友開始，兩個人沒有顧忌地聊各種沉重或輕鬆的話題，可以坦白地談著死亡、金錢、分手、第三者等等的事，也是因為這樣我們對彼此的認識很深刻也很輕盈，我想這是可以讓我們一起走下去的諸多能量來源之一吧——唯有清楚表達，不用猜測彼此沒有說出口的那些話，便是真正互相瞭解的契機，也因此才能適時地互相拉一把！

現階段我們兩個人正在各自收集地圖上的每一個地方 (無論是否出自自己的意願)，我已經橫跨七大洲了，George 只差一洲。而我們的情感已經一起走了十年，歷經了從朋友到戀人到夫妻的轉變，各自在遠方累積的經歷，讓我們可以互相給予對方不同的觀點；我們陪伴彼此這麼長的時間，其實已經走得很遠了，如果用空間來比，我們的關係大概已經走了五大洲了吧！而未來我們要走得更遠，我很期待我們的關係一定會有不同的可能性，尤其是如果有了孩子，應該會有些以前從來沒想像過的東西在心裡長出來，將我們的關係帶往自己從來沒想像過的地方！

想要一起去的地方

Ⓙ 目前我最想跟 George 一起去的地方是
古巴，因為古巴是一個一直在變的地方，
每天都以我們追不上的速度奔向另一個世
界。蜜月最想一起去的地方是坦尚尼亞的
桑吉巴（Zanzibar）島，那裡美的令人讚
歎。

Ⓖ 可是這次這樣史詩般的旅程結束後，
我好像暫時沒有想要一起去哪裡耶哈！硬
是要說的話，現在最夢幻的目的地是外太
空，我們要一起去外太空！

Ⓙ 桑吉巴可以啦，你可以躺在那裡一整
個禮拜，是真正的、完全的渡假耶，像馬
爾地夫那樣的地方耶。而且同時也可以滿
足我想去非洲的願望，我可以去草原，也
可以兩個人一起躺在渡假村裡，一起休
息、一起聊天。

Ⓖ 好啦……。這次去德州、阿根廷與南
極對我來說真的是很嚇人，也充滿挑戰
性——這是個未知領域，尤其是對我這個
比較沒有在到處旅行的人來說，是蠻艱鉅
的，而且不斷地飛行、不斷地在緊湊的
拍片時間裡生活著，有的時候會讓人很
疲憊。但是，也因此我們是很堅強的一
對——而且這次的旅程最後，我們倆結婚
了！

凱特文化 星生活 53

在世界的盡頭說：我願意
STARTING AT THE END

作　　者	Janet Hsieh 謝怡芬 & George Young 吳宇衛
發 行 人	陳韋竹
總 編 輯	嚴玉鳳
主　　編	董秉哲
責任編輯	董秉哲
封面設計	萬亞雰
版面構成	萬亞雰
攝　　影	郭政彰（南極部分）、林念儀（德州部分、阿根廷部分）
英　　譯	薛芷穎
文字協助	王詩情（Chapter部分）、羅山（Date部分）
行銷企畫	黃伊蘭、李佩紋、趙若涵
印　　刷	通南彩色印刷事業有限公司
法律顧問	志律法律事務所 吳志勇律師
出　　版	凱特文化創意股份有限公司
地　　址	新北市236土城區明德路二段149號2樓
電　　話	02-2263-3878
傳　　真	02-2236-3845
劃撥帳號	50026207凱特文化創意股份有限公司
讀者信箱	katebook2007@gmail.com
部 落 格	blog.pixnet.net/katebook
經　　銷	大和書報圖書股份有限公司
地　　址	新北市248新莊區五工五路2號
電　　話	02-8990-2588
傳　　真	02-2299-1658
初　　版	2016年11月
初版二刷	2017年01月
I S B N	978-986-93239-7-0
定　　價	新台幣399元

我的小三，她就是 Renee。她每天跟我在一起、有我家的鑰匙、知道我討厭那些菜、我不在時替我澆水、會跟我一起笑到肚子痛或是哭到沒有眼淚了。假如我失去了這位助理、經紀人、公關、保鑣、攝影師、助理製作、翻譯、隨身字典、知己、好友，我不知道我要怎麼辦。沒有她的參與，這本書不但不可能成形而且寫起來也不好玩。Renee，謝謝妳幫忙了這麼多。妳真的很了不起。

If I had a "mistress", it would be Renee. She's with me every day, has keys to my apartment, knows which foods I dislike, cries with me and waters my plants at home when I'm not around. I don't know what I would do without my assistant/ manager/ publicist/ bodyguard/ photographer/ production assistant/ translator/ walking dictionary/ confidant/ my friend. Without her, this book not only wouldn't have been possible, but it would have been much less fun to write. Thank you Renee for everything. You are nothing but amazing.

除了 George 跟我媽，最瞭解我的人就是 Tim 了。他十一年前「發掘」我，一定沒想到跟我一起拍片，他要忍受這麼多的頭痛、心痛、胃痛以及疲勞。我們一起經歷了很多事，有太多人生精彩故事可以分享！為了 George 跟我能在南極結婚，Tim 也是付出了最多的犧牲與協助。他讓我真正的明白了 Henry Ford 的名言：「相聚只是開始，保持團結才有進展，真正合作則是成功。」讓我們能再繼續一起成功往前進。

Other than George and maybe my mother, if anybody knows me better than myself, it would have to be Tim. 11 years ago, when he "discovered me" I don't think he thought he would have to endear all the headache, heartache, stomachache, and muscle-ache that he has working and filming with me. We have been through so much together and Tim has sacrificed more than anybody to make my wedding to George in Antarctica a reality. He has truly taught me what Henry Ford says so well, "Coming together is a beginning. Keeping together is progress. Working together is success." To many more years of success together!

國家圖書館出版品預行編目資料

在世界的盡頭說：我願意／Janet Hsieh 謝怡芬 & George Young 吳宇衛 著．
－－初版．－－新北市：凱特文化，2016.11 216 面；18×25 公分．（星生活；53）
ISBN 978-986-93239-7-0（平裝）

855   105018018

George 讓我見識到，什麼是勇氣。

　　給對方，無條件愛著對方，朋友啊，這需要勇氣。

所以　　　想承認，也不得不說，George 那兩粒贏過我了。

He really showed me what it meant to be courageous.

To give yourself 100% to somebody, to love them unconditionally.

That, my friend, takes courage.

So, as much as I don't like to admit it,

George has bigger cojones than me.